MacArthur Middle School

BROTHERS
OF THE
HEART

BROTHERS
OF THE
HEART

A Story of
the Old Northwest
1837-1838

JOAN W. BLOS

Charles Scribner's Sons/New York

Copyright © 1985 Joan W. Blos

Library of Congress Cataloging in Publication Data
Blos, Joan W.   Brothers of the heart.
Summary: Fourteen-year-old Shem spends six months in the Michigan
wilderness alone with a dying Indian woman, who helps him, not only to
survive, but to mature to the point where he can return to his family and
the difficulties of life as a cripple in a frontier village.
[1. Frontier and pioneer life—Michigan—Fiction.
2. Michigan—Fiction. 3. Physically handicapped—Fiction.
4. Ottawa Indians—Fiction.
5. Indians of North America—Fiction]   I. Title.
PZ7.B6237Br 1985   [Fic]   85-40293
ISBN 0-684-18452-4

Published simultaneously in Canada
by Collier Macmillan Canada, Inc.

1 3 5 7 9 11 13 15 17 19 F/C 20 18 16 14 12 10 8 6 4 2

Printed in the United States of America

Stephen's book

Contents

BROTHERS
OF THE
HEART

I

An Anniversary Is Celebrated

SHEM AND MARGARET ELLSWORTH PERKINS lived, in good health, to celebrate their fiftieth wedding day. Their children came, with their husbands, wives, and children, and the children of these children. There were friends and neighbors, dear and close, so it made a goodly number.

Tables with white tablecloths were set about the lawn. Chairs from the house were brought out, too, and placed in pleasant groupings under the shading maples and along the open porch. When winged maple seeds blew down, the children picked them up and laughed, perching them on their noses and peering above them to see.

Just beyond the white wood fencing, horses, harnessed to their buggies, reached for roadside tufts of grass and switched their tails at flies.

The photographer came out from town, a small man and precise. On the buggy's gleaming door gold lettering, in a circular design, gave the name and street address of his studio.

After the photographer climbed down, men gathered to assist him. First the box of photographic plates was carefully handed down. Then the camera itself, a large affair of wood and brass, with three splayed wooden legs.

Shy at first, the guests of honor were led to the center of the lawn and advised on the pose to strike. The photographer ducked beneath his cloth and eyed them through his lens. The couple hung there, upside down, the husband in his good black suit standing beside the wife.

"Hold it," cried the photographer, and everyone drew breath. Straight into the camera looked the blue eyes of the husband and the dark eyes of the wife.

"Oughtn't he to *sit?*" someone began to ask but was quickly hushed.

The wife wore a lightweight summer dress, long sleeved and full skirted, a small brooch at the throat. Her skirt spread wide where it touched the grass, but when they received the finished photograph, the tips of her plain shoes showed. Her large hands, restless in her lap, must have tugged it out of place.

Now the crowd flowed back to life. The screen door banged behind each one as the daughters and the daughters-in-law brought out hams and roasted chickens, biscuits and potato salads, pies of many different kinds, corn, and snapped green beans. The guests moved toward the well-filled tables. Everyone remarked upon the fortunate good weather.

The women had started early in the day before it got too hot. Now they were well satisfied with how it all turned out. A pleasant breeze had struck up, too, riffling skirts and tablecloths and showing, in the stronger gusts, the underside of leaves.

Then, as so many times before, someone asked to hear the story: tell about the two Pierres and how you carried money for the bank; how it was the day you met; how it was back then!

It no longer mattered which of them began. They had told it all so often that the disputes and disagreements had long since worn away. Seeing that his wife was tired, Shem took up the story.

"The road, back then, was a narrow path just wide enough for a wagon, cut between ranks of trees . . ."

II

Along an Early Road

THE ROAD RAN WESTWARD from Detroit, straight out to Chicago. Most of those who traveled it at that time were likewise going west. However, this was not the case with the particular wagon with which we are here concerned. A farm wagon, hooped and arched with canvas, it belonged to one Thomas Perkins, Esquire, the father of our hero. Once he had lived in Meredith Bridge, New Hampshire. He was then a fiddler of no small renown and had kept a farm as well. In recent years he had moved out West, taking his family. Between the cities of Cleveland and Ashtabula, on a lovely, fertile plain, he had made his homestead and started in to farm. Then he sold his new Ohio farm to buy a house in Millfield, in the State of Michigan. Again they must move on.

At first they had traveled westward through Ohio; then north for thirty miles or so on reaching Michigan. Now they were heading east. The route was somewhat indirect, for they had to round Lake Erie's western shore to reach their destination. They hoped they might achieve it soon: this day or the next.

Wearing a farmer's hat and smock, the Fiddler, as he liked to call himself, tried to keep an even pace as he walked beside the wagon. It was thus that he could guide his team, not the horses of the well-to-do, but a pair of oxen, nearly matched, reliable and strong. The wagon was loaded till it strained with all his worldly goods. Lydia, his wife, with their youngest child beside her, rode at the front of the wagon on the narrow planking seat.

It is not yet time to tell of his eldest daughter; she was not with them now. And Luke, his reckless, firstborn son? The boy had died some years before, might he rest in peace. He, who had been so spirited and strong, had dared one risk too many. It was so like him, the father remembered now, to prefer the color red! How he had teased and wheedled with his mother till, in the garments that she sewed, she let him have his way. The Fiddler put it from his mind. No grief or other mortal act would repair the loss.

Behind the wagon, by some several lengths, walked the Fiddler's crippled son. He was always described in this fashion. He was fourteen years of age.

It sometimes is the wanton way of boys to tear a leg from a spider or an ant and watch that unfortunate creature as it tries to make its way. It limps; it lurches frantically. The strong side carries all the weight, the weak side keeping up. You would think of such a thing, seeing the Fiddler Perkins' son, for the boy had been born with a gimpy leg, and every step was an effort toward an uncertain end.

The bards, they say, and the poets love the lame; and perhaps God loves them, too. But the poets never tell us this: that at the moment of the birth the eyes that ought give welcome to a child turn, instead, away.

Shem.

It helped that he had had a sunny disposition. Indeed, for the first years of his life, he'd hardly seemed to notice that he differed from the rest. True, in those days, his brother and older sister were always there to help him should he fall, or to boost him high on a barnyard fence to delight in the suckling pigs. His mother had taught him how to read, sparing the walk to school. And often, in those early years, the Fiddler'd taken the boy along to gatherings, bees, and raisings—wherever it was he played. It had been a happy sight, to see the glad-eyed little boy astride his father's lap. Then, in the year that Shem was six, a sudden, raging springtime flood had taken the brother's life. The father hung up his fiddle, and a shadow crossed the house.

It was after this, by some two or three years, that they'd gone out to Ohio. There the infant Annie's birth had cheered them for a while. The parents had smiled to see how Shem had lavished on the little girl the care that he had known. Already, through his tutelage, she could say her ABC's and do the simplest sums.

But there had been no time for lessons when they sold the house and farm and prepared themselves to leave. Such a pretty house it was! You could not ask for better.

"Where are we going?" Annie asked.

"Michigan," Shem told her.

"I thought it was to *Millfield*."

"Well, there, why did you ask me if you already knew?"

"It's Michigan *and* it's Millfield," she explained to her cornhusk dolls, a family of four.

It was hard for Shem on this corduroyed road whose logs, laid crosswise side by side, formed an uneven surface and were slippery with moss. The strain of it made him awkward, and from time to time he fell. Pridefully refusing to use a walking stick, neither would he accept to ride with his mother and little Annie. They'd have gladly made him room.

Shem.

He might have been a comely lad, with his dark hair falling across his face and the clear, light eyes of the English who were his ancestors. Now, however, his face was drawn and hard. The boots he wore were meant as an assistance, but more often caused him pain. They were the well-meant parting gift of an Ohio neighbor, a cobbler of some skill. As the man had observed correctly, they could not know when next they'd find a cobbler to make another pair. So he made the new boots extra large to fit the next year's growth. He did not stint on leather and he reinforced the sole. The boots were exhausting by reason of their weight, and the knitted socks Shem wore did not remedy the fit. Many times the boots chafed cruelly and, when Shem took them off at night, the dark-gray socks were bloodied.

Shem thought, as he walked along, there is nothing you can do. Everything defeats you, the distance most of all. Perhaps your mind runs freely, but the pace remains the same. One tree. One stone. This brown and faded grass. They vanish as you advance. Ahead there are so many others! How many trees? How many stones? How many blades of grass?

And why, he wondered, had they come out here at all? His father said it all was for the best. Had Ohio failed somehow to satisfy the Fiddler? The only thing that Shem could see amiss was a moodiness in his mother. It came in—and it lifted—like the mists from off the lake. Perhaps, Shem thought, it was being so far from home. Did she miss the house where they had lived so long, and all the family? But why, then, push on farther to the West? Why not go back East?

He'd overheard his mother once asking that very question: "Why not go back home now, Tom? It's all been such a while."

"No," his father had replied. "There are things best left behind you, and misery's of that lot. Out West where we're going now—why, they say that Michigan isn't to be beat!"

Shem recalled the day when it began. A stylish stranger, mounted well, had reined in at their gate post and asked was the Fiddler home. Suppose, Shem thought, he had said that he was not. Would that have closed the matter? But no, he'd bid him welcome. The man had city lots to sell and every one was a beauty, to hear him tell of it! He had printed drawings, too, which, when he rolled them out for you, you had to agree were pretty. He had a plan that showed the intended streets. The Perkinses, he thought, would do especially well to buy a corner lot and house, with a back lot to the river. He had then come down in price.

To the Fiddler, who often thought of luck, this seemed like nothing less. The Ohio farm had prospered, he reflected, but it never seemed like home. Then, again, a city situation might be best for Shem. It would offer work, most likely, start them out anew. Reasoning thus, he had signed the purchase papers and brought them home with pride. He'd seized his wife's both hands in his!

"City folk is what we'll be! How d'you do and how d'you do—" Recalling how they used to dance, he swung her 'round right then and there in the summer kitchen! "So glad to meet you, mistress!"

His merriment had startled her.

"Oh, Tom, do stop playacting now. Whatever's done is done."

That was several months ago. Now, in her dark-brown traveling dress, brown so as not to show the dirt, she kept her place in silence and stared out straight ahead. It would go better, the Fiddler told himself, once they were settled in. A journey such as theirs had been would have to be hard for a woman. For his son, too, he supposed.

"Shem, you want to ride?" he called. He knew the boy resented favors, but could not help but ask.

Shem heard his father call his name but mistook the rest. He thought his father needed him and hastened to comply. Thus began a sequence of events more lasting in their influence than anyone might have guessed. Just as they often said back then, you never know, when a thing begins, where it is going to take you.

III

A Friendship Is Begun

EVEN AS HIS FATHER WATCHED, Shem's foot, in its awkward casing, slipped out from beneath him and the boy fell to the ground. Appalled, and feeling himself at fault, the Fiddler ran to help. This left the oxen unattended and, because the road was narrow and the team of oxen wide, even a moment's inattention brought them all too quickly to the cut logs' ragged edge. Very softly, almost smoothly, the right-hand wheels of the heavy wagon slipped sideways from the roadway into the springtime mud.

"Haw!" yelled Mrs. Perkins. But it was too late. The thick mud closed around the wheels, and the wagon, listing and askew, came to a total halt. The oxen, feeling the uneven pull, lunged forward in their traces. It was all the wife could do to soothe and keep them quiet till the Fiddler returned with Shem.

Nor did the efforts of some hours relieve their predicament. What defeated them especially was the great depth of the mud. The spoked wheels sank more deeply and the Perkinses felt their situation worsen with each passing hour. They tried to lighten up the load, removing furniture, kegs, and sacks, and setting them on the road. They pried and pulled; they pleaded with the team; they knew, even as they did so, that one team of oxen lacked sufficient strength. The wagon, as it had come to rest, was very nearly parallel to the road itself. Unless they could get it moving through the mud, they would have but little hope of restoring it to the road.

The only comfort that they had—and small it was at that—was knowing they weren't the only ones to be caught this way. Lately every mile they passed was strewn with wasted goods. In chairs and chests and lidded kegs they had read the stories of others like themselves. The Fiddler ruefully recalled that he had, not long ago, counted up his blessings. Subtract a little now!

Annie heard the other wagon first. At first, when she sang out her news, they thought that she had made it up with her good imagination. But presently their ears confirmed what hers had caught much sooner. A wagon, traveling east to west, was now approaching theirs! The sounds were not to be mistaken. Tinware clanked and wooden wheels screeched against their iron fittings with each slow rotation.

Oxen lowed, and blatting sheep kept up a constant protest. Roped to the wagon as they were, they must duly follow after.

Because the forest was so dense, it was a while before the other wagon could be seen as well as heard. At last they saw it was led by a man about the Fiddler's age, a man who walked, as the Fiddler had, beside his plodding team. A girl with thickly braided hair leaned forward from the wagon seat, frankly curious. Beside her, emotions more contained, rode the wife and mother.

"Don't do more than you have to, now," the Perkinses heard her caution, to their great embarrassment. "And remember to be careful till you know who's there." But the man was striding toward them and the Fiddler put out his hand.

Ellsworth was the other's name, and, for a time, the men worked on alone, Shem joining as he could. The strategy, they soon agreed, was to try to widen out the road, then use the strength of the doubled team to move the wagon forward. Shem was assigned to finding fallen wood for the men to cut and shape. The girl, whose name was Margaret, watched him from the wagon seat, though she knew she should not stare. At last she had to ask.

"How do you think it happened?"

"I suppose," the mother said, "he was born that way."

"You don't think it was later on, something bad that happened, an injury or such?"

"No, not by the looks of it." The mother turned from her own inspection of the busy scene. "One ought to give him credit, I would say, for doing what he can out here, which is hard enough for the rest of us blessed with two good feet."

"If I were him, I'd hide," the daughter said.

"Why, what a thing to say!"

It was scarcely an hour after that that the women were recruited to hitch the teams together and guide them as they worked. The men, and Shem, would keep the wagon balanced—by guiding it with heavy ropes—until it found the road. This left Annie to amuse herself, and Margaret who, denied a part, felt angry and excluded. She knew she ought to mind the little girl. But instead her eyes kept going back to the crippled boy. How stubbornly he struggled! She admired him in his pride.

Giving it no further thought, she now reached out to grasp the rope that he had been assigned.

"No," he said, "I'm not in need of help. Why don't you watch Annie? That's fit work for a girl."

Let the braggart be, she thought, and resolved to keep her distance. "I hope—" she called and caught herself. She was going on sixteen. Much though he deserved it, she would not wish him ill.

Even with the doubled team, it was dark, and growing cold, before they got the wagon properly on the road. Clearly they would not travel on that day. But whoever was disappointed did not speak of it. The rig was whole, and no one had been hurt. They were fortunate.

Each of the families now withdrew to make their preparations for the evening camp. Fires were kindled, water fetched, kettles set to boil. They added meal to thicken into gruel. Beyond all else the fragrance, as it cooked, reminded them of home. Thus it both made the wilderness recede and called up poignant memories of all they'd left behind.

With the supper hour's close, the women began to tidy up and the men stirred from their separate camps to exchange the news: Was it true that Indians were abroad and likely to make trouble? Not since last year's treaties. These were just and fair, folks said. Of course, one never knew. What had they heard of the cholera? Was it bad as the year before? No, but folks were saying that the ague, or the fever and the chills, was already starting. Then, as their paths ran opposite to each other, each one asked the other about the road itself. Was it better up ahead? That's what one always hoped.

"Well," said Mr. Ellsworth slowly, "well, I couldn't tell you yes. But then, on the other hand, I hate to tell you no."

The Fiddler smiled at this report. He felt he'd made a friend.

Now he began to tell about the new house he had bought. He offered to show—he insisted on bringing out—the printed Millfield plat. Also, for he had it right at hand, the picture of the central square that the agent had imparted just before he left. It showed clean streets, well-lined with shady trees and edged with picket fences where luxuriant roses bloomed. Ladies with tilted parasols chatted with one another, so it seemed, and a buggy and some horses made their way around the square. An artful ribbon, looping over all, displayed the new state's motto.

The Fiddler was glad to translate, as had been done for him. "*Si quaeris peninsulam amoenam,* if you wish a fair peninsula, *circumspice,* look about you!" And the Fiddler waved his hand!

"Well, is that right!" Mr. Ellsworth was impressed. "A fair peninsula! Long as it's got good acreage that's good enough for me."

Before the sky was light next day they bid each other affectionate farewell, supposing they would never meet again, at least not in this world. The women leaned from their wagon seats to wave, but the trees closed in so quickly as they went their separate ways. With the passage of a few more days, the grass that was flattened where they'd walked stood up straight again. Then it was just the ashes of their fires that told where they had stayed.

Meanwhile Fiddler Perkins' wagon had passed the region of oak clearings, distinctly marked on the map he always carried, and approached its destination. The road was a good bit wider here and ran on level ground. Shem and his father walked apace, the latter being happy and much relieved that the smoother roadway eased things for his son.

"Shem, boy," he exulted, "we are almost there! We ought to see it peeking soon, and what a sight that's going to be, after all these miles!"

The Fiddler, you could plainly tell, was filled with his own excitement. Shem watched his father brushing down his hair, adjusting the collar of the coat he had put on, dusting off the elbows and evening out the cuffs. So will any traveler who knows that a difficult journey is nearly at an end.

The approach to Millfield lay across a bridge. Even Shem, who resisted his father's cheer, could not deny that Millfield's situation was a pleasant one. The town was set on a modest plain, crooked in the river's arm. It was wooded, but not excessively so, and First Street, running true to plan, bisected the area neatly. At a greater distance from the river, a second and less developed street ran parallel to the first. It was First Street that divided, north and south, to bound the central square.

This concluded any and all resemblance to the plat and drawings that had shaped their hopes. The loyal artist who'd depicted Millfield's charms had strayed, with good intent no doubt, to the hopeful side of truth. Here there were no picket fences. Or roses. Or parasols. In fact, there were no villagers about, and Millfield's mud-filled, barren streets were innocent of traffic.

Shrugging on his greatcoat as he came, a solitary citizen was hurrying toward them now. His name was Parker, Ezra Parker, the keeper of the inn. Had they not seen it coming into town? Well, perhaps they had not known that it was an inn. He also was an officer of the Millfield Bank. Would they *dine* at the hotel? They would be his guests. Had Mr. Perkins seen the *mill*? Already it was earning well, past all expectation!

"—and here," their self-appointed guide announced with satisfaction, "here is where the depot's going to be! Convenient, is it not?"

The Fiddler nodded, confused and overwhelmed. But then, thought Shem, one might as well agree. Not one tie was laid as yet and, until the rails were down, everything was conjecture.

Now they had arrived at the location of their home with its corner lot. The house was agreeable as to size, and the frame looked true. But the surrounding flower beds, prominent in the cross-hatched drawings, proved but another example of the artist's zeal. Around the house was ruined, rutted earth. Rough-cut stumps and fallen, uncut trees gave the site a grieved appearance. It was as if the construction of the house had been a violation.

"Tom," Shem heard his mother say, "surely there is some mistake? Show him where our lot is at—show him the plat, Tom, corner place and grounds! Here's the letter with the Bill of Sale! Tom, for all you paid they promised—"

From the wagon Annie called, "Shemmy, why are we stopping here? When will we be there?"

IV

A New Home:
First Impressions

THAT NIGHT a thunderstorm broke loose such as none of them could remember—it was that severe. Lightning flared, and doorway, and then window, blazed with a light rectangular and harsh. Blazed and stayed in the mind's impression, for eyes were held *un*blinking—blazed and left behind strange odors, past all natural burning.

Thunder pursued these bursts of light and was, at times, simultaneous in its violence of sound. The wind was terrible in its strength. It bent and racked and twisted trees made pliable by spring thaws. Yet some of them were stressed too much, and now and then a breaking branch gave notice of surrender.

The Fiddler's wife especially was terrified by the storm. Once, as a child, she'd been caught by such a storm. It was when she was in an open field. There was one large tree in the center of the field. (They always left a tree like that to give them noontime shade.)

Frightened, the child had run to it. Then she'd recalled that such a tree, tall, outstanding, and alone, attracts the lightning bolts. It was dark and slick beyond the tree. She felt that she was safe there but knew that she was not. Just as she had left the tree, lightning struck, exploding it all to smithereens.

Amidst the tumult she was flung against the ground. The lightning was around her, so intense it hurt her eyes. For minutes the rain poured blackly down, just that and nothing more. When the lightning came again it was at a distance. Crying, the child commenced to run. Her clothes, soaked through, were heavy, and they dragged her down. She stumbled, fell, and finally reached the house.

"Why, Lyddie! Whatever happened? Look, your new dress ruined, too."

It was the memory of this time that recurred so forcibly when there was a storm. Even if she was safe indoors, she would begin to tremble. She really could not help herself. She would become as frightened as a child in an electrical storm.

Awakened now, the household did not speak but wondered at this outburst; wondered at this untried land, struck so early in the year with thunderstorms of such violence. They huddled together, holding each other close until the storm was spent. The only furnishings in the house were the cornhusk tickings laid down on the floor. Time and time and time and time again, the empty strange interiors were filled with the awful light. It was hours before the storm abated fully. No one slept that night.

Later on, much later, they would learn that the storm that night was unusual, as startling to those acquainted with the region as to those who had just arrived. But that was only later.

MacArthur Middle School

For nights thereafter the Perkinses fell asleep wondering if another storm would strike and, if that should happen, what damage it might do.

* * *

LETTERS TO MISS SOPHIA PERKINS. THIS IS THE OLDER
DAUGHTER TO WHOM REFERENCE HAS BEEN MADE. CALLED SOPHY
BY THE FAMILY, SHE HAD BEEN SENT TO THE LOWELL MILLS AT AGE
15 AND HAD NOT REJOINED THE FAMILY IN THE ENSUING YEARS.

FROM SHEM TO HIS SISTER

Millfield, Michigan
April the 17th
1837

Dear Sophy, as presently I am not employed I had thought to write to you of what we have found here. We traveled quite comfortably from Ohio, save for the last some miles of which the roads were very bad. Millfield is less established than we had thought having not so many houses built (about 27), side walks not laid on any street or part, building of depot not commenced, &c, &c. There is a saw mill and a grist mill, also a bank and inn. Nearby is a printer, and an establishment where they make a fine grade of pearl ash. This is where Father worked at first, and whatever else our worries we have good and plentiful soap! Some people here work at other occupations such as brick. There is a small store as well.

Most of the houses are frame and board construction. If any thing, there is too much wood. What is not used in building is burned by day and night. Our neighbor tells that when he built his house he did so by the light of the very fires by which his land was cleared. How often this is the case I do n't know. Our eyes are often sore. This is from the smoke & that is a certainty.

Our house is built two storeys high, a common fashion here. It is to have a full porch (not built yet) and rooms up stairs and down. Windows had glass in them all ready. Father has ordered a cooking stove. It is said to be safer and more excellent in results than our present use of the hearth. It is v. expensive, $36, but he is determined that we shall have the best.

There is no school or teacher. Mother teaches me rhetoric and logic; I have arithmetic and geography from Father; both bedevil me day and night to correct my spelling. They say I will be glad but I have yet to see it. We read the Bible every day, some, and two times on Sunday. I have read nine chapters of Mr. Dan'l Defoe's *Life and Strange Surprising Adventures of Robinson Crusoe.* Have you read it? It is very good. It is the second time I have read it. I teach Annie some times. It is hard for her to be patient.

Well, that is all I have to say. In the two places I inquired for employment they gave the positions to others. I hope this finds you in good health. Please write and tell us how you are. Ever your affect[n]ate brother,

Shem Perkins

On the road we had met a Mr. and Mrs. Ellsworth of York State (Genesee Co.). They have a daughter, Margaret, and, I believe, no others. They had intended buying land near Bronson but now they are here with us.

* * *

Millfield, Michigan
April 17, 1837

Dear Sophia,

I could not let a letter go to you without I had carted my mile. Some days past we were joined by another family. We had met them on the road. They had intended farming farther west but were not successful in obtaining land. Ellsworth is their name.

We have been here five weeks now. Your father is well employed—$1.25 a day. The climate here is as good as you could hope. There is no church, school, nor RR yet. Nor side walks. They have got a good bridge (new) across the river. It is shallow. Our house is nearly complete—very nice—but when it will be done I do n't know. We have v. much to do. There is a good 1/2 acre cleared. It is not uncommon to see six or seven teams together for this purpose.

Well, I guess that is all for now. Remember to be kind to those who are less fortunate than yourself and in all you do be diligent. Any thing worth doing is worth doing well. I would that we might see you soon again, but I do not now see how. Perhaps after we have been here some time I will come to see you.

Ever your loving mother,
(Mrs.) Lydia E. Perkins

* * *

There were not, in Millfield at that time, many boys Shem's age. Those there were worked mostly with their fathers, to learn the family trade or business, as the case might be. In due time they would join their fathers—which is how WILLIAM PLATT, DRY GOODS became WM. PLATT & SONS.

The Fiddler, being newly employed himself, had nothing

he could offer Shem in the line of work. Tasked with preparing the garden plot they intended, Shem, in the end, spent much of his time at home. And what could one say of this? For Shem's sake they had given up the farm. And here they were now, city folk; and Shem it was who spent his days as a farmer might! It wasn't that he had not tried. But, as Shem had noted in his letter, in the places where he'd asked, preference had been given those who were sound of limb.

When Shem was small he had sometimes asked about his crooked leg and foot—his wrong foot, as he called it. His mother would smile and put him off, distracting him with a sweet. Now he felt he had to know this first truth in his life.

He felt there ought to be a reason, believed that she must know. "Why?" he asked her. "Why?"

"Shem," she said, "there is nothing more to say. I beg you, Shem, for God's sweet sake, and mine, not to ask again."

He could not keep away from it and asked repeatedly. Then one day she turned on him, taking him aback.

"An answer's not like butter in the churn, pound away at it long enough and something's sure to come! When will you let it be, Shem? It's just God's will, is all."

Around the question silence grew. But the question was still there.

Meanwhile the ladies came to call, and Mrs. Perkins was hard pressed to make the cakes to serve them with with what she had on hand. Neither had she honey nor maple sugar to put to them as sweet.

The young and pretty Alice Howe was among the very few

whose visits were returned. She was the printer's little wife, and perhaps she reminded Mrs. Perkins of her distant daughter. She and the printer, the girl explained one day, had married when quite young. She had been rather reckless, she supposed. Her parents had been that relieved to see her settle down! But the printer held some controversial views and expressed them in his paper. Not only did he favor abolition, he was an atheist.

Once, on account of his opinions, he had been warned of violent acts by those whom he'd offended. It was then the printer and his wife had come to Michigan. It was then a territory, and slavery was prohibited by the Northwest Ordinance. She agreed with him on that: no one should hold slaves. As for religion, she didn't quite share his views; but she was proud, she added fiercely, that he said what he believed. Thus far, she was glad to say, Millfield had accepted her and though it kept an eye on him, there had not been any trouble.

Mrs. Perkins hadn't known what to say, she was so surprised! As she said to the Fiddler later on, the printer had seemed so quiet in his ways and the girl was so well-spoken.

Throughout this time they had not often seen the Ellsworth family. Then, one day, Mr. Ellsworth himself appeared. The work of clearing land was slow, slower than expected. He'd heard that Shem was not employed. The question he had come to put was this: would Shem work for him? Mr. Ellsworth could not offer wages. Instead he would consider that he owed a just amount of labor at Mr. Perkins' need. Such arrangements were quite usual with those hard up for cash; equally typical of those years was that the father freely placed an agreement on the boy.

The Ellsworth land was on the western edge of town. Good for farming, it was not too far away from the planned location of Millfield's station stop. A dwelling built by a previous owner enabled the Ellsworths to live there till their own house should be built.

The story went that the cabin they'd acquired had been built to satisfy the original owner's wife. She'd wanted her house, however small, to imitate in its design the stone homes of her girlhood. Thus it was wider than most cabins but a lot less deep. Even as the cabin was being built, the wife ran off with a mason. All that remained of her brief sojourn was a house with an extra window on each side and a story worth retelling in the cold of a winter's night. Mrs. Ellsworth liked the windows. She said they gave more light.

Shem had heard the story often. Now, he thought, he would see the house, *and* he had employment! It was almost funny, the way it all worked out.

Always afraid that he might fall, Shem was cautious as he made his way along the slippery bank. The river itself was luminous, filled with the morning light. In the mist there were little threadlike swirls. You could hardly see to the trees on the opposite shore, though the river was not that wide.

Shem wore his usual square-cut smock, trousers, hat, and boots. He carried a piece of cornmeal cake and his mother's parting words.

"You'll be wanting a bit come midday," she had said. "And

it's none for them to be giving you food to eat. No one here has more than what they need. Don't forget that, Shem."

That was just an hour past, and now Mr. Ellsworth could be seen, awaiting his arrival.

"Margaret's hitched the team," he called as Shem approached the gate. "We'll go down directly," he explained as he joined Shem on the path.

But Shem's mind fastened on the first: *Margaret's hitched the team?* What was that to mean, he wondered. He had not long to wait.

"You two," Mr. Ellsworth added, "would have a lot in common, being so far from school. Not that you mind, I don't suppose—" He smiled at Shem in a friendly way. He was wanting to be kind. But, from the way the daughter bent her head, Shem began to realize that he was meant to work with her— a girl!—all the livelong day.

V

The Wilderness Is Claimed

ANYONE WHO PIONEERED THE REGION would recall in later years how they labored in the woods, converting verdant forest to productive farms. Never mind that these were noble trees! They felled them and they burned them, and the cleared land slowly grew. When the wind blew toward them from the fires, the smoke it carried stung their eyes and throats. Injuries were frequent; some recovered, some did not. Often weeping, widows, wives, and sisters drove the teams of oxen, pulling the reft stumps from the ground, after the trees were cut.

Shem and Margaret, like the others, worked as long as it was light and often did not speak. Always arduous, often filled with pain, the labors they had been assigned seemed to have no end. As time went on and the work still loomed immense, expedience made them gird the trees instead of felling them. This cutting of the vital bark meant that the tree would die. Crops could then be planted at the base for, leafless through the summer months, a girded tree did not block out the sun. Next autumn they would come again to cut and clear such trees.

As the trees were taken from the land, its contours were revealed. Thus did they discover a curving, gentle slope. At its foot was a pretty running stream; at the top, a level site. Exactly there, said Mr. Ellsworth, he would build their house.

Although they had worked hard before, they must now accomplish more. To extend the hours of the working day, Shem was obliged to leave his home long before dawn broke. At sundown, when their own work ended, he and Margaret would help her father build a blazing fire near the new home's site. Then they would be dismissed. Mr. Ellsworth, staying on alone, kept the fire for its light. Night after night he dug his cellar hole. When he had made it large enough he braced it well with logs.

After he had sufficient timber cut, the raising would be held. Once the frame and ridgepole were in place, he could go on alone. He thought that with any luck at all he ought to have it livable before it came on cold. He wasn't meaning finished; just so it could be used.

It often seemed that the labor of one day was continuous with the next. Shem, who must walk the extra miles to town, sometimes wondered if it was any use—to be dismissed, to make his way to home, to sleep, and then to rise again to resume the work. Day after day, weary and in silence, Shem saw Margaret to her door and then continued on.

Once, as they neared the Ellsworth cabin, he stumbled as if to fall. Margaret put out a hand to help, but he caught himself.

"Are you all right?" she asked him.

"It's just the leg—it's short, you know, because the foot is wrong."

"No," she said, not knowing what to say. "No, I hadn't noticed." They'd never mentioned it before, as if by an agreement.

"Truly?" He grinned widely. "I guess most people see it and they think of that the first."

"Shem," she said, astonished and dismayed at his misunderstanding, "how could I help but notice? I only meant to say, I guess, that I guess it doesn't matter."

It mattered to Shem, tremendously. Whatever he might do or think or say, he was Shem, the Fiddler's crippled son, the boy with a gimpy leg. And the best that anyone could say was that it was God's will.

* * *

PRINCIPAL TEXT OF LETTER FROM THOMAS PERKINS, ESQ., TO
HIS DAUGHTER.

July 27, 1837

Dearest Sophy,

I take this opportunity to give you an exact account of our present situation. We are well, thanks be to God, and hope you are the same.

Our house is none too large, dear Sophy, but we are accommodated nicely. We have got a cooking stove, $36, and it is the most convenient thing you ever saw. There is only one other stove such as this in the county. I have 1/2 acre of excellent ground for a garden. It is near the house. The first employment I got was with Mr. Ballard, making pearl ash. The first day I was there I was offered $1.15 a day, 5 ¢ past agreement. Soon, my master being still more pleased, I commenced work in his corn mill, $1.25 a day, and there hope to remain.

Your brother looked very hard for work but on account of his condition none was for hiring him. Now he helps a neighbor clear his land, and I may expect a change of work for this, one day's work for two.

This is a very pleasant place. I think you would do well to come here also and if you do it would make me very happy. I will send directions &c. for your travel.

If you should contrive to come it would be well to bring clothing. Here it is very dear. Shoes are cheap. We are able to purchase commodities but prices are high from the roads being very bad. We hope this will soon be corrected by the Rail Road.

Do not send any thing by freight as it is most uncertain if it will ever arrive. The lawlessness is a terrible thing, esp. in Buffalo and Detroit where the ships put in. If you do know some one who is coming, let him bring cuttings of currants and gooseberry, if he can. Also seeds for vegetables and what he can of flowers.

Your mother has not been feeling very well but you are ever in her thoughts. Soon she will write I think. Well, I guess that is all, dear Sophy. May the good Lord bless and keep you and may we meet again ere long, hopefully in this world.

Your loving father,
Tho. Perkins, Esq.

* * *

For a house to be raised successfully, it was generally considered that lumber, whiskey, and good, strong men were equally important. Of lumber get as much as would be needed; of whiskey get as much as possible; of friends and neighbors, near and far, all that could be summoned. A raising was an occasion to which everyone came who could. It was social as well as useful, and it lasted into the night.

"There's a raising at the Ellsworths'!" was the word. By wagon, buggy, and on foot people began arriving early on the appointed day. To start the work, each section of the frame was assembled on the ground. Then, many men working together, it was hoisted into place. The process required skill as well as strength, and the timing must be exact. Mr. Ellsworth asked another to oversee the work.

"Heave-oh-heave!" the cry rang out! Each man strained against the frame's great weight. The outermost beams were supported in position as the whole was lifted from the ground, and the process was then repeated. Again and again they inched it up, using sticks called "mooleys" to support it as it rose. When the frame had got too high to reach, these crotched sticks were used to move it, as well as keep the place. When, at last, the vertical was achieved, the section was fastened into place, and they started on another. Frame by frame they raised it till the four sides were in place. Then the rafters were fitted into place and the ridgepole last of all. Each time it seemed miraculous! In space that was nothing but air before, the shape of a house appeared.

It would, of course, take the work of many days to fulfill the frame's bright promise. But now Mr. Ellsworth had no doubts, and Mrs. Ellsworth, as she watched, was careful not to cry. It seemed to her that this joyous, happy moment marked the end of a journey, the longest of her life. She reached out a hand for Margaret, who was standing by her side. The girl had looked so beautiful today! She was glad that she had let her wear a brooch that she'd worn as a girl.

Fiddler Perkins cheered with the other men. It was good to be there with them all, and good that his son had taken part in the hard work of the day. On the other hand, he could not help but think of the days back in New Hampshire. That was when they used to say that you couldn't raise a house or barn unless the Fiddler Perkins played when it came time to dance.

Here they knew he would not play and kindly had not asked. The fellow who was tuning now could play the notes all right. But that was not the same. The Fiddler remembered with a smile that Shem had thought the tunes were in the fiddle. Once he asked his father how he let them out.

For reasons unrelated to each other, the day of the raising marked the end of Shem's work with the Ellsworths. For it was shortly afterward that the Fiddler was stricken with the ague, the fever and the chills. He was the last of Millfield's men to be taken ill that summer, and it took him hard.

One can hardly tell of the region at that time without a substantial mention of the fever and the chills. One reads of it in every letter and all the histories.

* * *

FROM: *Michigan Pioneer and Historical Collections,*
V, 300-304.

We could always tell when the ague was coming on. . . . At first the yawnings and stretchings stole upon you so naturally that for a while you felt good in giving in to them; but they were soon followed by cold sensations, that crept over your system in streaks, faster and faster, and grew colder and colder in successive undulations. . . . There you laid shaking in the frigid ague region for an hour or so until you gradually stole back to a temperate zone. Then commenced the warm flashes over your system, which increased with heat as the former did with cold, until you reached the torrid region, where you lay in burning heat, racked with pain in your head and along your back for an hour or so, when you began by degrees to feel less heat and pain. . . . Getting back to your normal condition, you felt relieved and happy.

* * *

One notes that these early reports are touched with a certain laconic humor. "He ain't sick," people were wont to say, "he's just got the ager."

As the swamps were drained and cultivated, the mosquitoes decreased in number, abating the disease. Quinine was presently introduced, and soon the ague, chills and all, passed into history. But back in 1837, when Thomas Perkins first took sick, the ague was still rampant. As has been said already, he got it worse than most.

His attacks came every other day, instead of every third day, which was much more common. Also they left him extremely weak—"weak as a baby," Mrs. Perkins said, and she ought to know. He had to give up working at the mill. The worst of it was that, as they lived in town, they needed to have cash money. They had counted on his earnings, and these completely stopped. These were troubled, worried weeks that they lived through day by day. In the midst of it all came Sophy's letter, a letter so full of happiness it seemed to mock their misery, which of course was not intended. The letter was written in August, and it came through in good time.

* * *

LETTER FROM MISS SOPHIA PERKINS TO HER FATHER, THOMAS
PERKINS. TEXT NOT GIVEN IN FULL.

23 August, 1837

Dear Father, this leaves me in excellent health and hoping you are the same. I received your letter of the 27th inst. and hasten to reply. Do not look for me to come! I continue to find good wages as a tutor and will send you all I can when the means present themselves. I do believe that the Mr. Hall whom you will know as the brother of Chas. Hall, and the uncle of my friend Catherine, soon intends removal to your whereabouts. I will inquire can he bring the seeds that you have requested. I hold you in my most tender affection and think of you every day. . . .

In September a college for females is expected to open here. I am in correspondence with the intended directress and daily await her notification that I may attend. My fees will be $52 for board & the first quarter tuition $16. This I can pay with my wages, which I am saving toward that end.

It grieves me that you are far from me but all is for the best.

Kiss Mama for me, and Annie, and tell Shem that I think of him and hope his health is good.

I close with kind remembrance and affection, and am ever your daughter,

Sophy

* * *

VI

A Well-Commissioned
Errand

DURING THE TIME the Fiddler was most sick the only help the
Perkinses had was Mr. Ellsworth's change-work time, owed to
them through Shem. It made the boy feel better, some, that
this went back to him.

With his mother's help he gathered what corn had ripened
and harvested the one small stand of wheat that they had put
in. He bagged the grain and took it to the mill. The only boy
amongst strong men, he listened to the others. They had to
raise their voices to be heard above the tumult of the stream,
the horrendous noise of the mill wheel, and the tumbled roar
of a million kernels as they ran the wooden chutes. It was a
satisfaction to them all that the first year's yield was good.

"By God," they said and meant it, forgetting their own
pain.

The grain, returned to them as meal, swelled the rough-
sewn, loosely woven sacks. So plump they seemed about to
burst, each one, at the slightest touch, gave off flour dust in
clouds! It billowed thickly about the men as they pulled and

tugged the bags and tied the tops with rope. The odor of milled grain is sweet. This, along with the flour dust, clung about their persons as they started for their homes.

It was at the mill that Shem first heard the rumors about the bank. Millfield's was said to be a wildcat bank, chartered within the letter of the law but dangerously unsound.

"Few and evil were the days of this banking," Mr. Chief-Justice Campbell was to write, "and the history of the system ... would be humiliating but perhaps profitable reading now."* The banks were the ruin of many in those days, and not only those who owned the banks (and might be said to have brought it on themselves) but depositors as well. Often these unfortunates learned too late that the florid, printed notes with which the banks competed could not be redeemed.

On a sunny autumn afternoon the very Mr. Ezra Parker who'd welcomed the Perkinses to town stopped to speak with Shem. At first he inquired of Mr. Perkins' health; he had heard that he was poorly. It then turned out that, on the bank's behalf, he wished to speak with Shem.

Perhaps, as he now elaborated, the boy had not been quite aware that recently the Millfield Bank had had a bit of trouble in making good its notes. Another bank, a sister bank, had gladly helped them out. Now Fate had played a little trick and quite turned the tables! Shem would certainly understand that it was therefore Millfield's turn to show its friendly spirit.

---

*Cited by Bela Hubbard in *Memorials of a Half-Century* (New York: G. P. Putnam's Sons, 1887), p. 92.

On Thursday, which was three days hence, would Shem transport to the Highland County Bank some needed certificates? With horse and wagon, both to be provided, Shem could easily make the trip in a single day. Mr. Parker said that he himself would go, but it might be awkward for a man in his position to play the messenger. All Shem had to do, once there, was wait until some government men completed their inspection. Then he would return to Millfield, bringing back a packet from the Highland men. What could be easier, he asked? And for this work: twelve dollars!

Shem thought at first he had not heard it right. Twelve dollars for this errand! The bank and village were not far, and besides he was not asked to walk but would have a wagon. Well, he would go, no doubt of that! Who would not do the same?

Mr. Parker had just one more thing to ask. Nothing would be said of this, either before or after. Indeed it would be better if—here he tipped his beaver hat—Shem would not remember who it was that spoke to him.

The hardest part, Shem thought next day, was keeping it a secret. Oh, if he could tell his mother! Let her start, this very day, to be proud of him! Perhaps, he thought, if everything went well, they'd call on him again.

One hopes—no, more than that, *expects*—that the day of a special enterprise will dawn bright and clear. In fact, Shem woke to heavy rain, the kind of late September rain that strips the maples of their yellow leaves and leaves the landscape dimmed. As he dressed Shem wondered if his errand would be postponed. (He'd come to regard it as an errand, but with what reward!) Fully dressed, and his morning tasks complete, he made his mother a brief excuse about some promised visit to the Ellsworth farm. He warned that he would not be home till evening; they were not to worry.

"Wait a bit," his mother urged. "Surely the rain will slacken?"

"A bit of rain won't hurt," his father said. He knew that his wife was uneasy, like a cat, in the slightest turn of weather. Shem silently thanked his father and left before more was said.

By the time he reached the appointed meeting place, Mr. Parker and another man were awaiting him. They had hitched the horse, a bay, and in the bed of the wagon was a nail keg and some blankets.

Mr. Parker's easy words answered the unasked question. "As long as you'll be going there," he said, "I thought as you could take along these few things for my friends. You'll not have to trouble yourself with them. This is what they're wanting."

Now he took from underneath his coat a strapped and buckled leather case of the kind used for dispatches. "Papers," he said vaguely, "for when the inspectors come. Do not let them from your sight; this is what my friends need most, and I'd hate to disappoint them. I'm sure you understand me, Shem. Well, get on with you!"

Shem placed the packet on the wagon seat, saw that it was conspicuous, and dropped it to the floor.

"Good boy!" Mr. Parker called, and waved in a friendly

manner. Shem carefully placed his booted foot so that it hid the packet where it lay, and signaled to the horse.

The road soon came upon a wooded stretch, and Millfield was left behind. Although the rain had let up some, the trees let loose great showers as he passed. It was not a pleasant day.

As he went along, he passed a number of settlers' cabins, each one in its clearing. A few inhabitants waved to him, taking him for a farm boy on a farmer's errand. Shem returned the greeting, hoping to look the part.

He found it hard to judge the time in the gray, unchanging light. But presently the road improved itself, and the homesteads came more closely. He supposed that this meant a settlement was near, and he hoped that he was right.

It was scarcely more than a crossroad though; not much of a one at that. Of its half-a-dozen buildings, one was distinguished by a roughly painted sign that proclaimed THE HIGH- LAND BANK. Like the other buildings it was a cabin made of logs, and the men who issued from within seemed casual in their welcome. Shem handed on the leather case, and the small tableau dispersed. He then had nothing more to do but ensure that the horse was cared for after the morning's drive.

There is just so much attention one can give a horse. Shem soon came to the end of it and, puzzled that no one was about, found a seat where he might wait. Shem noted that the case he'd brought now lay open on the table, revealing printed certificates, documents, and blank notes.

At the back of the structure he could see a second and smaller room. Its opened door was equipped with a heavy lock and this was its only access. Ledgers filled the tier of shelves and here, in well-constructed kegs, were the bank's own stores of gold.

There next ensued an odd charade as the sturdy keg that Shem had brought was hefted and poured off. Beneath a layer of common building nails were more gold coins than one might have thought to see in an entire life!

All at once Shem understood the ruse. This, and not the leather case, was his most valued freight. Now, when the government agents came, they'd be inclined to grant approval to a bank that clearly had such large stores of gold.

"What we're doing here, you must understand, is all for the good of the bank." One of the men had noted Shem's frank stare and offered an explanation. "It's just that we were caught a little short, and what with the inspection—." Turning to look at Shem, he said, "It would have worried everyone, and what would be the use to them of naught but needless worry? So that's when we sent to our Millfield friends, and much obliged we are. Soon as the inspection's done, back it goes to Millfield, and no one is the wiser. Nor the worse for wear."

Shem must have looked uncomfortable at this, for another now spoke up.

"What do they know in Washington what it's like out here? Beaver hats and away we go! The way this country's growing now, you can't *make* rules in Washington that'll go for everywhere. It stands to reason to bend the rules so as to make them fit.

"Don't you worry, son, it will be all right! And many's the

soul who would thank you from his heart if he knew what you'd done today."

It was precisely what he'd done that worried Shem the most. But the man who had spoken seemed a very decent sort, and sincere in what he said.

After that they did not pay Shem much mind. They shared the midday meal with him, for which he was duly grateful. Then, as the afternoon wore on, it became apparent that the government inspectors would not come that day.

Shem, as is hardly surprising, did not sleep well that night. The narrow bench where he'd sat in the afternoon was less than adequate as a bed, so his sleep was fitful. And what had his parents made of it when he did not come home? Especially his mother, who was like to carry on.

It simply had not occurred to him that there might be a delay! Now that it had happened, there was nothing he could do. Rather, as his mind reversed upon its track: there was nothing he could do now that it had happened.

He tried to direct his attention to the spending of the money. A new grub hoe, they needed that! But would his mother, he wondered now, have gone out to the Ellsworths' to see if he was there? He sighed—and found another way to lie. He hated to think she had gone there in the dark, worried and alone.

Next day the bank inspectors came. They were younger than Shem had expected and seemed rather bored. The documents, notes, and coinage were examined—including the gold that Shem had brought—and the bank received approval. Hands were shaken all around; the men remounted swiftly and were on their way.

At least the need for the building nails had been genuine! They kept the nails and returned the gold, the documents, and the case. No events of any sort disturbed the journey home.

VII

Runaway!

SHEM HAD BEEN PAID with two bank notes, one for two dollars, one for ten, and both of them had been issued by the Millfield bank.

He studied the notes with open admiration as, limping heavily with fatigue, he made his way up First Street to his parents' house. He hoped that they would be at home. He thought he would give each of them a note, but which to give to whom?

"Where in God's name have you been?" His father's words shot out at him as he crossed the yard. Whatever Shem had imagined had not begun like this.

"I had a job, sir," Shem replied. "Proper work. For pay." He handed the notes to his father: proof. It was not what he had meant at all. He felt it going badly, and he could not put it right.

"Shem, I asked *where have you been*, not what did you earn. I would like you to answer my question and to do that first of all."

"That I cannot say, sir. I have promised not to tell!"

"Shem! I am your father!"

"Sir, I may not say."

His father looked down briefly at the notes he held. "The Millfield Bank? Is that where you got these?"

"Yes, sir, that is right."

"Then I will tell you what I think. That you have worked for crooks and thieves; that you have kindly helped them out, going against the law! Dammit, Shemmy, don't you ever *think*?"

"No, sir. Yes! I mean, I did! I only thought to help us out, you being sick this while. We need the money, that I know, and it *was* a lot of money."

"*Was* is right," his father said, and he tore the lovely printed notes from top to bottom, side to side, and let the torn scraps fall. "*Was* is right, Shem, and you mind: just because I've come down sick doesn't mean that you can do whatever it is you want. I'm still your father—"

"Yes, sir, yes—"

"Look up when you're spoken to!"

"Yes, sir, yes; I hear you."

"Is that the best you have to say? Well, this is what I have to say: I don't need the goddamned help of a goddamned cripple."

Intention has nothing to do with it. No more than deeds can be undone, words like this, once spoken, cannot be recalled.

What it does not heal, time hardens. Neither the father nor the son knew any longer what it was he wished the most: to forgive or be forgiven. When, much later, they tried again to speak, they came to the nub of the argument, straight to its stone-cold heart.

"What did you do, Shem, and for whom?"

"Sir, I may not say."

Shem now felt that to Margaret and his father he was nothing but a cripple. Oh, they would deny it, but was it not the case? Her words so gentle, his so loud, amounted to the same. Why then wait till it should come up again, as he now knew it must? They'd do better, Shem convinced himself, free of Shem the cripple who never seemed to please.

Shem, when he decided to run away, fixed on a Sunday morning. Everyone then would be at the morning service and he would refuse to go. They would not persuade him, things being how they were.

Ought he to leave a message of some kind? There was nothing he could tell them, having no destination. Later, when he'd news to tell, that's when he would write to them; till then, let them wonder. Annie? What of Annie? He had not been kind to her of late, and all her corn-husk boys and girls were, she said, so naughty that she didn't know what to do.

He did not cross the river by the bridge but rather headed north. The road, as it climbed from the narrow river valley, led through largely unclaimed lots, marred by the wild and boggy land so typical of the township. By dint of all the wear they'd had, his leather boots were softer now. Still, he was aware of them as he undertook his journey.

When, at noon, the sun stood overhead he ate the bread

and sausage he had brought, regretting there was not more. Later on, remembering, he would be appalled: one never ate the last of one's supplies. No matter how little there was left, a man could survive on a small next meal, but not on none at all.

In another hour's time he came to higher ground. Shem guessed he was nearing Daunton, although he was not sure. Would anyone in Daunton know that Millfield's Fiddler Perkins had a crippled son? Would he be recognized? detained? his parents notified?

So much for vanity! If anyone saw him passing by, it pricked no interest. He followed the road as it led through town and dipped down toward the river. Soon the burnished oaks and ash, brilliant in October colors, closed in overhead.

George Howe, it will be remembered, was a printer and an atheist, the husband of Alice Howe. Because of his beliefs, he had not been at the service on the day Shem took his leave. No one thought of questioning the printer—people seldom sought him out except in the line of business—nor had he come forward. Still, when he heard that Mrs. Perkins, sick as she was with worry, could not either eat or drink, his heart went out to her. Although past efforts had not been well received, the printer now put on his woolen shawl—October could get chilly—and went to the Perkins' house. He told them how he'd watched Shem from his shop, puzzled because the boy had seemed to carry a well-packed, blue-striped sack. The boy, he thought, had not seen him; he had not called him back. He was not the sort to meddle and the boy had looked composed. No, there could be no mistake. You could always tell Shem from afar by his awkward gait.

To know that Shem had gone of his own accord relieved his mother greatly. She'd begun to fear it was Indians that had taken him. One heard of that too often. Wasn't it but a few short years since Black Hawk had his war? In her gratitude she resolved to resume her waning friendship with the printer's wife.

She remembered, now, how needlessly they'd worried the night that Shem had ridden for the bank and not gotten home. Why, they had not slept the livelong night for wondering what had happened! That was partly what made Tom upset! She wished he'd not been so severe, tearing up the notes and all, and Shem so proud of them. It did no good to think of it. Perhaps, with what the printer had just said, Shem would soon be home again and all would be forgotten. That would be the best.

Meanwhile, it had been discovered that three hundred silver dollars had vanished from Millfield's bank. When Mr. Parker also vanished, it was generally believed that the company Shem had served had called on him once more. Some gave out that they thought he might have tried to find his sister Sophy. No one guessed the truth.

On the third day of his journey, Shem had hailed the eastbound stage and presented himself to the driver. He said he was a poor, bound boy and most unkindly treated. He said that he'd been more than sadly used, was even now pursued. Shem had not had much to eat. His pallor was convincing and the kindly man, persuaded, had offered him a ride.

So, with luck to aid imagination, or perhaps it was the other way around, Shem had been carried directly to Detroit, and it had cost him nothing. There he had found employment of which we shall shortly hear.

VIII

An Old Acquaintance
Reappears and Is Introduced

SEATED AT HIS SMALL, HIGH DESK, feet concealed beneath it, neither Shem nor his handicap was conspicuous. He had obtained a clerk's position and spent each day at his dockside desk, filling his ledger's pages with tedious detail. Shem, as he bent over them, was attentive and absorbed. He listed names and goods and shipments; value and date of arrival. He no more saw the waterfront, where he worked, than he dwelt on thoughts of home.

A disembarking passenger, caught in the swirling noisy scene, would make no note of him. Even if that passenger hailed from a small New England town and had known Shem as a boy, there was nothing to catch his eye. Equally, it was not to be expected that he be recognized. For the Uncle Jack of Shem's New Hampshire friend had worn a full and wiry beard, redder than his hair; the passenger was clean-shaven. Too, the man whom Shem had known had worn a farmer's woolen smock or, in working at the mill, was dusted white with flour. The traveler to whom our story turns cut a finer figure. Indeed, he was dressed in the latest fashion, such as one expected of those come from the East.

Who can know how it might have been had it been otherwise? If Shem had recognized his old friend's Uncle Jack? If he'd been recognized? If Shem had been persuaded to return? If Uncle Jack had brought assurance that the son was safe? Those who have played cat's cradle know that the selfsame length of string assumes many different patterns as it passes back and forth. So each question shares its substance with the last but resembles it not at all.

* * *

FROM THE PERSONAL NOTEBOOKS OF JOHN HALL, ESQ.

Fare	New-York City to Buffalo	$6.25
Luggage	at $1 per hundred wt.	1.00
Fare	Buffalo/Detroit (rail, coach, and voyage)	3.00
Luggage	at 1/2 dollar each barrel bulk (more than required but could not obtain partial space)	1.00
Accommodation + meal	(Detroit)	.57
Cartage	to Millfield	2.00

* * *

The John Hall, Esq., who was otherwise Uncle Jack, had arrived that afternoon. He was bound for Millfield on account of its good report, and he it was whom Sophy had entreated to deliver her packet of seeds. He had not many household goods, being a bachelor; neither had he brought with him all that he possessed. For what he had, the wagoner's fee seemed exorbitant!

"Two dollars just to Millfield?" he exclaimed. " 'Tis all I paid to bring the lot clear from New York State!"

"But, sir, the roads, they are very, very bad! You cannot believe how bad they are, the roads!" This was true, for he *did not* believe, but he also had no choice. He agreed to pay the price.

Having done so, he was much relieved. Now, in the early evening hours, he felt himself quite free. After the days on board the ship, it was good to walk about. Detroit was Michigan's largest port and, in 1837, its capital as well. He was curious.

Cart and wagon traffic jammed the narrow waterfront area and its adjacent streets. Here shops competed fiercely for the patronage of travelers, of those intending settlement, of traders and of boatmen. In the summer months, when steamers plied the lake, it was not at all uncommon for close to a thousand persons to debark in a single day. Some had hopes of high financial gain; others came with humbler expectations and a wish to share the future of this newly admitted state.

It was to this latter group that our John Hall belonged. He had always felt a bit constrained by the liens that others placed on his independent state. But his elderly parents, rich in years, had died, and his brother, long a widower, had married again, and well. In short, with no one needing him, it was time—and then some—to look out for himself. He had cast his eye on the western states, thought of Ohio for a bit, and chosen Michigan. It had joined the Union this past March. Mere months old, he reflected! Why, it was just a baby, and he hoped as full of promise!

The journey had been a smooth one, and John Hall was pleased. He had heard well of Millfield and was confident of employment. Although he had always lived alone, he got on well with people. A miller's trade required that, and it had never troubled him to accord with the tradition. In time he hoped for a gristmill of his own. He would search till he found the best location, build a house there, build a mill. It would have to be close to the river for the mill, and also to the road. For the present, he thought it would suffice to find a single room for hire and make do with that. He wasn't too particular, just so it was clean.

Two days after landing in Detroit John Hall arrived in Millfield. He found the Perkins' house without delay, and through the Fiddler's intervention it was arranged that he would use the cabin on the Ellsworth land where the Ellsworths stayed at first. As John Hall himself observed, it was nothing if not practical to save on cost and labor by using what was there. What the Ellsworths had found cramped for three, he reveled in as spacious. Whereas they had felt the loneliness of the woods, he had them for neighbors. What he could pay in rental, they could use as cash. These considerations having been duly taken, the bargain struck proved fair. He was, as they noted, a most agreeable man. Perhaps, having had no family of his own, he had learned to accommodate himself to the families of others.

They soon began to call him Uncle Jack. Indeed, it seemed that settling on that term was pleasing all around. With all the old kin left behind, there was something comforting about a borrowed uncle.

During one of his earlier Millfield visits, and after he'd delivered the seeds that Sophy sent, John Hall came to mention Amos Edwards' death. He'd been talking with the Fiddler and Mrs. Perkins of people they'd known in common back in Meredith Bridge: Charles Hall and his new wife Ann, his daughters, Catherine and Mattie, and Daniel, who was her son. They spoke of the Shipmans and the teacher her sister married, and hadn't that been a time! And then he came to the merchant.

"Had you known him," John Hall asked, "who lived down to Piper's Woods?" 'Twas said to be an accident, but there were few who doubted that he'd gone and blown his own head off, hunting squirrel one day. Perhaps they'd heard already?

No, they had not heard. Because those who wrote them from the Bridge knew that Amos Edwards' name put Tom into rages. Had the good Jack Hall not known of this, or had he just forgotten? Had he felt that these old friends ought to know? It was hard to tell.

If the visitor saw her catch her breath, at least he gave no notice. Tom—thank the heavens!—made no fuss. The talk flowed on to other matters, leaving her alone.

* * *

LETTER TO MRS. CHARLES (ANN HIGHAM) HALL FROM MRS. THOMAS PERKINS. FRAGMENT ONLY.

... We have learned through the Mr. Hall who is your husband's brother of Amos Edwards' death. It has taken me very hard. In the times before I married he and I had courted. But the days of our youth cannot be recalled and whatever tales you may have heard I pray you to discount.

* * *

The gossip to which the Fiddler's wife refers had centered on an episode of some years previous. Once, when the Fiddler had chanced to be away, Amos Edwards, bent on an innocent errand, had happened by the farm. A summer storm had threatened. At the wife's behest he had brought the cattle in and stayed till the storm was spent. By then the road was flooded and overrun. He had stayed the night. It was not a secret. Was the boy not there as well? Indeed, the wife had told her husband of her recent caller on his return next day. Had she betrayed more pleasure than she meant? He became so angry! It did take her by surprise. Nor would anything she said assuage his great emotion. No, he must go straightaway to the Bridge and settle with the merchant. So doing, he had called attention to the very happening that had otherwise gone unnoted. Meredith Bridge, predictably enough, had then begun its whispers about the old romance. Like a fire started in the brush, such talk is easily started, and notably hard to stop.

The net result was that the Fiddler and Mrs. Perkins, distressed at home and mortified abroad, had soon removed to Ohio. They gave out that the farm was dry as, subsequently, they would say that they had moved to Millfield for the sake of their crippled son.

The odd thing was, or not so odd, that learning of the merchant's death took each so differently. To the wife it was a deadly blow, even as Shem's disablement, even as Luke's death. Why had these bad things happened in her life? What might happen next? For the Fiddler, on the other hand, it put the past to rest. He wished that he could tell his wife how beautiful she was.

IX

The Youngest One in the Party

Now had November's silver light replaced October's glow. In the ledgers that Shem kept, the number of entries, week by week, visibly declined. On days when a steamer was expected to arrive he wore thick gloves with the tips of the fingers clipped. That way he could hold his pens, and he wrapped himself with blankets while he kept his dockside place.

Close to the end of such a working day, when hands and feet were icy, a boy who was even younger than himself appeared in search of Shem. The messenger, too, was muffled and wore blankets as a cloak. Shem, he said, was wanted at the office. He would lead the way.

Having no idea what yet might be in store, Shem took along his ledger and his pens and his stoppered ink. They started out walking side by side, but the messenger soon led by many yards. Halfway across the open square, he seemed to become aware of this, for he turned and halted until Shem caught up.

A large gray building, set back from the docks, housed the

company's central office. Hallways led from the entryway to unmarked labyrinths. Shem saw no way to distinguish them, but his guide seemed confidence itself and led as swiftly as Shem could follow through corridors whose wooden floors magnified their footsteps' sound and filled Shem's ears with the dismaying echoes of his own uneven tread.

"It was Mr. Prentice wanted you. He'll be over there."

As suddenly as the boy had spoken, so he turned and reversed direction, leaving Shem alone. He shrugged and removed his blanket and attempted to smooth his hair. He knocked on the door that had been pointed out and entered as directed.

The wintry sky beyond the single window was darkening and severe. It was dark enough to reflect the scene within and showed a man of slender frame bent above a simple desk crowded with documents and ledgers, very like Shem's own. On the floor beside the desk were ragged piles of ledgers and thick books. Behind him a fireplace framed in wood gave both heat and light.

It was in this somber situation that Shem was offered a new position: clerk to a trading expedition bound for the wilderness. The venture was unusual and risky. But the season had been a poor one and now the lakes would soon freeze over. Then, until Spring, there could be no further shipping and only further losses for the company. On the other hand, a successful expedition might bring a bit of profit when it was needed most.

Then the man explained to Shem that he had been selected on evidence of his loyalty and the merit of his work.

Throughout the extended time of his employment Shem would be fed and lodged.

"And pay, sir?" Shem inquired.

"Pay to depend on the success of the expedition. A just remuneration to each one. Not large perhaps, but just."

Shem nodded, at a loss for words, and surprised by this turn of events.

"Have you nothing more to say?" asked Mr. Prentice sharply. "Could a cat have got your tongue?"

Shem's mother used to say the same! It rather took him by surprise to hear it spoken now.

Shem said clearly, "Thank you, sir. I am much obliged."

"Good," said Mr. Prentice. "You may expect to leave Detroit on the third day of December."

"Thank you," Shem repeated.

Mr. Prentice dipped his pen in ink, ending the conversation. He had not guessed the boy would be so young, and with one lame foot besides. He hoped the boy would be all right. He began to check another set of figures. There was nothing he could do.

During the six weeks of his service, Shem had been lodged with the other clerks in a building maintained by the company expressly for this purpose. Here, for the first time in his life, were others as disabled as himself. Some, like Shem, had been handicapped at birth while others had clearly suffered a disabling injury. As each boy found in each other boy's condition a reflection of his own most hated aspect, they tended to be isolated, even among themselves. Still, lame or maimed as the case might be, they did have this in common: the other boys avoided them as if their disabilities might somehow be contagious.

Now, outranking all the rest, Shem had been selected for a new and exciting post. He was pleased that he'd been chosen. Yet it also seemed to signify to him that, as a cripple, he could hope for nothing more than success in the life of a clerk. This it was that spoiled his mood and of which he was not aware. Blaming his ill-humor on a thousand other things—from the weather to the boorishness of his friends—he managed to depart from the city of Detroit without having written to his parents or feeling the slightest pangs.

There were, as Shem now understood, two parts to his journey. Before setting out for the wilderness, he would go to Mackinac Island in the straits between Lake Michigan and Lake Huron, two of the five great lakes. This little but strategic island had been named by the Indians. The Englishmen who explored the region had transcribed its name as *Mackinaw*; meanwhile, due to French phonetics, *Mackinac* was the rendering of their French counterparts. Small but persistent, the confusion seems to echo the struggles of great nations for lands that are not theirs. But the final syllable rhymes with *paw*, however it is written.

Shem was to report to a Mr. Beaubien on reaching Mackinac. As the leader of the party, Mr. Beaubien would have assembled the supplies and the beads, pots, cloth, and blankets they would use in trade. At Mackinac he would find a boat and boatmen to propel it. Then would begin the journey's second part to its final destination.

* * *

3 Nov., 1837   Snowed quite heavy this morning. I do not know what we shall do if winter commences early. We are not prepared.

Sund.   Visited with Mrs. Ellsworth. They are very kind.

14 Nov.   Had hoped we would have word from Shem by now but the stage has come and went and nothing for us there.

* * *

Shem left Detroit on the fourth day of December, on one of the smaller steamers of the company's fleet. The departure had been delayed one day due to the inclement weather. The steamship's course lay northward: first along the Saint Clair River, and thence to Huron's waters.

None of the men aboard the steamer were assigned to the expedition in which Shem was to take part. They felt no need to engage the lad in talk, nor did he invite their friendship. They saw him as a lonely youngster, more aloof than surly. He shunned their company at meals and seemed to resent the most casual of questions about family and home. In their high-topped hats they walked out on the deck; Shem, finding its surface treacherous, spent much time below.

Observed or not, the shoreline as they passed presented a forest of giants. Here were elm and beech and linden and towering tulip trees. The maples' spread was enormous. The oaks, less gnarled than those inland, grew to majestic heights. Gradually, as they traveled on, the evergreens that crowded to the shore became more prominent. Pines that reached to one-hundred and fifty feet were not unusual. The forest, as they saw it from the lake, was dense and green and dark. It made their noisy, smoking boat seem paltry and intrusive.

On Monday, the tenth day of December, six days after setting forth, the sure contagion of arrival struck the little boat. By afternoon they glimpsed the island: Mackinac, with its settlement and fort and the white sand of its beaches.

Although the sun made the wintry day quite pleasant, the bay was full of ice. They learned on arriving how bitterly cold it had been. Last night the thermometer had dropped to two below and the wind direction made them think that worse was to be expected. They were far, now, to the north.

In other seasons there would have been more traders, also many travelers seeking quaint and distant scenes. But even at this time of year the island swarmed with profiteers and soldiers, adventurers and officials and zealous missionaries. Indians and whites, Englishmen and French, and citizens of the United States mingled on Mackinac's Market Street and in the several communities of that well-trafficked island.

Shem, still gloomy and preoccupied, hardly seemed to notice. Indeed, it is something of a testament to the degree of his lonely self-absorption that he saw so little of the place and took so little notice of his surroundings there.

The days from December tenth to twenty-first were spent in engaging the necessary men and equipping the expedition. Shem learned that the Frenchman who was to be in charge had spent much time on Mackinac and knew its leading citizens and the nuances of trade. Beaubien, as he was called, was said to drive hard bargains, but none that were unfair.

The first man hired was Zozep, a canny woodsman whose first years were spent with his Indian mother. Through her he knew about the forest things that no man, coming there fully grown, could possibly discover. Again, through his mother, he knew the Indian tongues and was a storyteller. He knew a use for everything and, with solemnity, would explain why the water lily blooms and why the smoke of the manitou's pipe is seen in Indian summer. He told how a man, leg caught by a falling tree, used his knife to amputate the leg, and crawled home. And survived.

Shem would listen fascinated, reviewing the stories in his mind and knowing better than to ask which of them were truthful and which were merely true.

But Zozep's skills were in the woods. Beaubien needed, among his men, one who knew the lake as well as Zozep knew the forest. It proved more difficult than he had supposed to meet this requirement. When time at last pressed in on him, Beaubien took on, despite misgivings, a man who was said to lie when sober and fight when he was drunk. But he clearly knew the lakes in every mood and was utterly without fear. His preference was the bark canoe, but he'd also sailed the small lake schooners and the so-called Mackinac boat. Where strength was a commonplace attribute, his was legendary. Like many another boatman, he was notably short of stature and powerful of build. His name, Pierre, revealed his heritage, or at least that of the father.

Then, on the day before they were to leave, another man appeared. Beaubien, feeling instant trust, hired him at once. This man also was named Pierre, but he was as kindly as the other one was not. As Good Pierre and Bad Pierre they were known thereafter.

Beaubien felt better in his mind once Good Pierre was hired. Although he had no worries about Zozep, the first Pierre, now Bad Pierre, was the sort who might give trouble. Too, Beaubien was very much aware that the clerk who'd been assigned to him was younger than the usual and severely lame as well. He wondered why they'd chosen him and assumed they'd had good reason. They could not now turn back.

They left the island on December twenty-first, winter's shortest day. It was rash, perhaps, to head onto the lake at this time of year. But a trade in fur was not for the faint of heart and the company's survival might depend on this expedition. Delayed too long already, they must make what haste they could.

At first their choice of a Mackinac boat had let them sail before the wind and they covered fifty miles or so in the first day and the next. Then the wind had shifted, and the lake's calm surface broke. Thereafter they depended on the oars, and as the boat was fully loaded, progress greatly slowed. Displaying his mode of leadership, Beaubien assigned himself and Shem to fair turns at the oars. It was also at this time that he decided that they would not press as far as they had intended. Instead of a location on the Grand, they'd winter on the Manistee, using an abandoned shelter built some years before. The difficulty he foresaw was that they'd now be at a distance from the lands where the Indians maintained their lines of traps through the winter months.

Shem had watched the others as they worked, taking the huge oars lightly in their hands and singing as they plied them in perfect unison. Their blitheness led him to misjudge the hardship of the work.

The oars were heavy, cold, and rough. Shem's hands were quickly blistered. Each day undid the healing of the night and there followed days when simply to grasp the oars brought agonies of pain.

The wind was against them steadily. Beaubien was worried because their progress was so slow. They started each day early and they seldom stopped till dark. In cold and darkness they would make their camps. A tent would be pitched for Beaubien and Shem; where the other men would lie, they heaped layered branches topped with evergreens. But each of the five had a blanket of his own. In that they were democratic.

When they stopped with light to spare, Zozep would vanish directly, and no one called him back. Time and again, from these sere and vacant woods, he'd return with meat to eat. For Zozep was in his element here, his quick mind noting where a fox had made its den and where a marten courted. Here the ground was firmer underfoot, once a trail had run this way and—there! a rabbit crossed it. Slowly now, and quietly. Ah-ha! my little fellow, I have got you now!

This meat would be a good addition to the usual evening meal of ground corn cooked with water. Whatever they ate at one day's end formed the morning ration of the succeeding day.

After a while, Shem realized that when hare was added to the meal, his was the largest share.

"Why?" he asked Zozep.

"So that," the ready answer came, "your legs, which sorely need it, may receive the strength from his."

"As well give me fowl that I might fly," was Shem's disdainful answer.

Zozep shrugged, but Good Pierre spoke up. "Unless you think of something better, you'd do well to eat it. Those boots you wear so faithfully, they help not so very much."

Shem blushed, but he apologized. Nothing more was said.

Not long after this exchange Good Pierre pulled some clean cloth from his pack and offered a length to Shem. Perhaps he felt that the painful hands had gone on long enough. He showed Shem how to bandage them for the night, first covering the blisters with a heavy grease. It was evil-smelling stuff, but Shem hardly noticed. Pierre's big hands were gentle and his treatment worked.

Despite their recent trials and disappointments, throughout the last part of the journey the dramatic beauty of the passing shore could not be ignored. High sand bluffs adorned with slender grasses fell sharply to the lake. Pines that had slipped from the heights above lay extended, roots exposed, still vigorous and green. White gulls rode the currents of bright air even as the boat itself was borne across the waters of the lake to a last encampment.

Shem was taking turns now with the rest. When they reached their destination, his hands were thickened, tough, and brown. Running an unfeeling thumb over unfeeling fingertips, he smiled with satisfaction.

X

A Difficult Decision

THESE VERY WEEKS of Shem's advancement were extremely difficult for the Fiddler and Mrs. Perkins. Loneliness assailed them, and the loss of many hopes brought on a deep and melancholy state that could not be relieved. The Fiddler's health was much improved, but the mill could offer no employment at this time of year.

Winter. The sun, when it shone, hovered in the sky, a pale yet radiant circle that held and disturbed the eye. But most of the days were gray and dark, and as the old year waned and turned, the cold and dampness deepened. It filled not only the larger spaces of drafty barns and residences but the hidden, intimate structures of the furnishings. Tables, chairs, and bed frames grew icy to the touch. Floors were so cold they *gave off cold*—and all this with the nearly continual heat of the brand-new cooking stove and the hearth fire burning.

They did not have so much of snow, but what had fallen thawed and froze, until gray ice was everywhere, for it never melted. People said that the heaviest snow was more than likely to come in March; spring began in April.

* * *

LETTER AND POST SCRIPT SENT TO SOPHY PERKINS
AT ABOUT THIS TIME.

Millfield, Michigan
December 28, 1837

Dearest Sophy, I hope you have not thought ill of us, not having written in all this while, nor supposed things worse than they are truly as they are bad enough. I must tell you also that your mother is very low. Since Shem left she has scarcely slept or ate and is downcast in her ways. It is a terrible thing to see. At times I am fearful harm may come. You know what I mean. Annie has been often sick and consequently fretful. We have been obliged to Mrs. Alice Howe. She has helped. Sometimes A. has stay'd with her, it is so bad here. I do n't know what I shall do with none to help at planting or at harvest, Shem being willing enough at least, but now he is gone. I have not the wages to pay a hired hand.

Land in now $3 per acre in most places. Taxes are also high. Sophy, I would take it kindly could you contrive to leave your situation till your mother's health is restored. Also, tell them at the college to return what money you have payed. That will pay your fare.

I am in hopes of seeing you as soon as weather permits. Your mother too, I think.

Next year the train will come to our door, I hope. For the

present you must take the stage after you reach Detroit. I am ever, your loving father,

Thomas Perkins, Esq.

Deare Sophy, Give to them that want. I can write. From,

ANNIE

* * *

The Fiddler had not told his wife of this latest letter. When they had Sophy's answer, that would be time enough. Meanwhile, save for the loyal Alice Howe, few entered the stricken house. It was hard on the Fiddler to be obliged to her, and he knew too well how little there was there to cheer a visitor!

"Is Shem with Luke now?" Annie asked one day. They said that was a dreadful thing to say and heaped on her reassurances, which they did not half believe. In truth, as the weeks and months wore on, it was harder to console themselves by finding innocent reasons why they had not heard from Shem. By now the Fiddler had to think that unless great harm had come to him, the boy had probably fallen in with bad company. As the first of these ideas was too terrible to consider, he fastened on the second. Little by little it grew and was embellished. At last he saw Shem nested down with wicked men whose ill-got gains might well corrupt a boy. And suppose, he began to worry, Shem incurred great debts? Would he then be responsible? He, the Fiddler, could not pay! He saw his home and holdings seized up by the law. His thoughts were running on, he knew, and scaring him the while! With effort he trimmed the wilder notions, and he never told a soul. But the fears and doubts persisted and they wore away at him.

During the next and sleepless nights, the Fiddler came on one thing he could do to protect himself. On the other hand he thought it might be misread, with painful consequences. Wishing there were someone in whom he might confide, turning it this way and that, he at last made up his mind. Before that very week was out, he made his way to the printer with a notice he'd prepared. He wanted it in the paper so that everyone would know.

I no longer am responsible for my son, Shem Perkins. Being free to trade and act for himself hereafter, I will not claim his earnings nor be responsible for his debts.
SIGNED: Th. Perkins, Esq.

The next week it appeared in print, lodged between a bookstore's notice and some small announcement.

Sadness overcame the Fiddler when he saw it there. This he did not understand; for although it had been a difficult decision, he had finally felt quite certain of what he had to do.

The notice, painful to its author, attracted few other eyes. Although Shem's disappearance had caused a stir at first, except in his own family it had largely been forgotten. His departure, like his presence, had not been an aspect of their lives to affect them much.

There was one exception. Margaret Ellsworth thought of Shem and wondered if she could have helped and why it had gone so wrong. If she had made him happier, if she had made

XI

Put to the Test

THE ACCOUNT OF SHEM'S WILDERNESS SOJOURN rests on his own writings. Especially the letter, which began as a mistake, should not be judged too harshly. Left behind by Beaubien and the others, alone and snowbound in the cabin, Shem was convinced that he was facing death and not without good reason. Apparently he felt that his parents ought to know of his final, desperate trials, for he wrote to them at length. The letter covers four loose sheets torn from the ledger, closely filled with his neat clerk's writing. The rest of the volume is not now extant, having later been returned to the company's office.

The notebook, also offered here, was revised in later years. By then the writer could provide a lighter tone, a more adventurous style. Indeed, Shem often appeared to see himself as a Yankee Robinson Crusoe! But that was only *afterwards*, the fact of his survival having dispelled his fears.

As we read these pages the central question is: how would Shem acquit himself amidst adversity? Till now, although he'd faced hard times, Shem and his situation were balanced

in his favor. Three times his wit had reinforced his luck: first
with the stage that brought him to Detroit; second, in his employment as a clerk; third, and last, in the matter of his selec-
tion for the trading party. In the events ensuing, Shem would
be put to the test.

* * *

February 9, 1838

Dear Father and Mother,

I have not written in some time and in these circumstances
do not know if I shall see you more. It is very bad just now. I
am in the wilderness, alone, & if I survive till Spring or not is
anybody's guess.

According to the tally stick, to which I have attended every
day, it is 19 days I have been alone and I have seen neither
white man nor Indian. I am able to have enough of fish which
I obtain by fishing through the ice in the Indian manner. My
sole companion is the wolf who comes nightly to my door to
eat the scraps I leave there when I conclude my meal. I lie
awake until he comes. This is not from fear, as you may suppose, but rather to know that he is there: we are all that live
here, we inhabit this wild place.

These woods are desolate. They are without oak clearings
or any other form of help to their habitation. We had thought
that Fortune smiled when she led us here. Now I think that, if
she smiled, it must have been for knowing that she'd played
so neat a trick.

I shall now contrive to tell you of my life since the day I set
foot to the road. My first destination was Detroit, to which
place I was speedily conveyed by means of the eastbound

stage. I readily found employment as a clerk, and sent up thoughts of gratitude for all the hours I had spent at spelling and penmanship. I was housed with the other clerks and so had no complaints. Some of them had come from overseas, but most were good New-Englanders, as I announced myself.

Detroit is not a very agreeable city. They have had the cholera there two times in the last five years. In one part there are mansions with avenues well layed out. The river is very fine and wide with settlement on both sides. It affords an excellent harbour to all manner of ships.

(2)

I was pleased to be selected as the clerk to a trading party. We went by steamer to Mackinac Island, where we layed over a full two weeks. I did not see many Indians, as they leave these lands in winter and have other hunting grounds. A Mr. Henry Schoolcraft is the Indian Agent there. There were some who felt we took great risk to set out at this time of year, and the boatmen were displeased that they'd miss their celebration of the New Year holiday. Mr. Beaubien prevailed on them, for we were late already. I think that this affected the party's humour. Later, when the men grew restless, they could not be contained.

We started out prettily enough but several times must needs encamp until the wind subsided. For this reason a journey which might have been made in four or five days took us twice that long. Most days we went twenty or thirty miles. Had we been able to go with sail we might have travelled faster. Several times the water came over the sides, threatening to swamp us and being very cold. However the men were excellent and we suffered no misfortune.

I think I have not told you yet who was in the party: in addition to myself there were Beaubien, the trader, Zozep, who is half-Indian and an excellent woodsman, and also two Pierres. They are as different as men can be in their character. Both of them are boatmen of the usual French extraction.

The men slept open to the sky but Mr. Beaubien and I were given tents in which to lie, so there is some advantage in attaining to a clerk's position. Each of us had a single blanket and, depending on our situation, used it divers ways. At times we spread it under us and, at times, it sheltered us from excessive blasts of wind. Or it might be a covering, in the more usual manner. Often, in the winter months, it is used as a garment over all the rest one wears.

We ate as well as might be expected, of small game as we caught it and the corn we had in store. Usually what we made at night sufficed for the morning meal as well. Some times we went without.

(3)

We arrived in this place on the last day of December. We found much snow and the river frozen over, on account of which we could not attempt our intended destination, which was still quite distant. We knew we should be inconvenienced as to trading but we had no choice. Also there was a cabin, nice and usable, although needing some repair. It was built a few years since by the loyal crew of a schooner which was savagely wreck'd nearby. Their captain was severely injured and the men being very fond of him would not leave without him. They remained here till he died. The cabin itself was well known to our men and I believe that Beaubien had seen it once before. It was excellent to our needs. The first night here we had much to eat and drink. Whiskey is not allowed in trade, but every party has its share, and had not Beaubien promised to welcome the New Year?

After we had stayed here several weeks, a restlessness broke out. Also Mr. Beaubien was wax'd that no traders (Indians) had come to challenge us in trade. Therefore it was determined that he and the others would set forth, travelling as far as, but not beyond, the Grand. Taking food and goods to give in trade, they left with fervent promises that they would soon return. For my part, with such cheer as I could muster I bade them all farewell.

I had wished to go with them. However the snows were heavy and the journey lay over land. They warned me I should fare but ill with snow shoes and my boots. Also it was necessary that some one remain at the cabin. Zozep set out traps for me and assisted me to clear some paths so that I might reach them despite the depth of snow. So it was that the portions were assigned. I had scarcely seen them out of sight but that Zozep returned once more with a final rabbit. It was with sad, heavy hearts that we parted once again.

Now I must tell you of some thing else. You will recall my small French coin that Luke had given me, for luck, in the summer before he died. I had kept it faithfully, no matter what befell. One night, while we sat together, I had told the story and displayed the coin. After the men had left that day, I discovered that it was gone. I am certain now that Bad Pierre took it from me that last night as I lay asleep and trusting. But no more.

(4)

It is now eight days since I layed down my pen. During this time I have been quite ill and some times in despair of my life.

For two days I was helpless as a babe and could not go so far abroad as for fire wood. Nothing to eat but meal, uncooked, which I mix't as best I could with water from melted snow. I think I might as peacefully have died had not I heard my forest friend in the darkest hours of night as if in remonstration. I am even now extremely weak. It is bitter cold.

I think of you all most tenderly, especially our mother, and hope that Father's recovery has made him whole and well. Tell Annie I hope that she is good and tell Sophy, if you write to her, of my predicament.

Your son,
Shem Perkins

God willing I shall return to you when the weather is once more fair.

* * *

It was not until the letter was complete that Shem came to realize the folly of his act. He had no means for its dispatch, no post to send it by. He had now been twenty-eight days alone. He noted the full moon at night. It frightened him to realize how confused he'd been. What he did not recognize was that undoubtedly he had become confused because he was so frightened.

During these nights the wolf did not appear. Presumably Shem, as his situation worsened, had neglected the nightly ritual and the gifts of food. If Shem at times was aware of this changed behavior, he was too preoccupied to engage in a sense of loss. What Shem did not know, of course, was that the wolf had turned elsewhere and been satisfied. There was a consequence to this. But the story outruns itself.

In all the accounts he was to give thereafter, Shem did not elaborate on what happened next. In his journal there is only one remark. *I became very drunk.* On the other hand, it suffices.

Despite the regulations forbidding its use *in trade*, every expedition—New Year's night or no—had whiskey in supply. As Beaubien had put it once, "Shem, there are some problems in this life which simply are not soluble save in alcohol!" So he had laughed and poured himself a measure. "Here's to the world, Shem, and to hell with it!"

And so, weeks later and alone, the boy had done the same. "Here's to the world, and to hell with it," he said. The sentiment appealed to him. He drank to it with a flourish.

The drink must have seemed, to his unsuspecting palate, shocking in its strength. "Here's to the world, and to hell with it," he gasped. "Here's to the world—and to hell with it."

Silence received his voice.

When Shem's writing continues, it no longer takes the form of a letter to his parents. Rather the document exists out of a need to substantiate the triumph of survival.

The opening is abrupt.

* * *

FROM THE NOTEBOOKS OF SHEM PERKINS (UNDATED):

I knew now with a certainty they would not be coming back.

On the day I recognized this fact I became very drunk. Neglecting my chores, I remained in this condition for several days and nights. I awakened because the fire had gone out and solely for that reason. Sick and stuporous tho' I was, I was forced to recognize that if I failed to exert myself, and soon, I should freeze to death.

It further became quite clear to me that had I had but slightly more to drink, or had the cold been slightly more severe, I should never have awakened.

I judged it to be midafternoon. The cold, I knew, would be more intense as the night drew nigh. Not much time remained to me; I must have a fire and I must have it soon.

The very urgency of these thoughts succeeded, at this juncture, in clearing my foggy brain. My flint and steel, having lain with me undisturbed, I found readily in my pouch. However I was soon presented with new cause for despair.

In my oblivion I had burned whatever dry wood I had had at hand, giving no thought to replacing it with logs set near the fire to dry out in their turn. Here was a cruel irony, I thought. Surrounded as I was by woods, I was like to perish for having none to burn. The standing dead wood close enough to reach, I had long since taken. All that I had was sodden wood, logs I might pry from the icy snow outside, or fresh wood cut from trees. As well attempt to ignite these with a spark as hope a fish hook might succeed in bringing down an oak.

I seemed to have awakened only to slowly die. I briefly considered my prospects for escape through the snow-filled woods. But had my friends not told me, very plain, that, on account of my condition, I would not be able to travel across the snow? And even if I made my way, defying their prediction, how far could I hope to travel with neither map nor compass nor good knowledge of the land? Within the cabin, what lay there? Cold increased by more cold as the night came on.

My feet were already painful with the cold. Yet I knew that they would soon give up the pain and that the very loss of pain was more ominous and grave than the pain itself. Cold would meet cold within my veins and, thinking on my poor dead self, I commenced to cry.

My grief became quite generous. I cried for myself, my father, and my mother. How saddened they would be to learn of my small and lonely end! A thought of my sister, Sophy, released yet fresher tears.

I cried for being about to die, and I cried that life was hard. Arms upon my puncheon table, forehead resting on my arms, I cried although too old to cry, and had no wish to halt my tears; nor could have, had I wished it.

I presently became aware I must relieve myself. It seemed that I was farther from extinction than I had supposed.

After the dark disorder of the cabin, the clear lines of the native trees, the clear, cold air, the new-laid snow glistened before my eyes. I saw that the world was beautiful and felt that I would live.

On returning to the cabin I noted with surprise that my recent tears had vanished as a dew. The table had absorbed them, its wood being old and dry. Here, then, was my rescue! I knelt and, through now grateful tears, gave thanks to Providence.

* * *

He'd be able, he thought now, to restart the fire before the daylight failed. First he took apart the table, saving each nail carefully to straighten and use again. Then he made a heap of shavings and one of slivered wood. Gently, gently, he used his flint and stone. At last a shaving caught. Shem leaned forward carefully, cupping it with his hands.

A sudden gust swirled toward him. He must have failed in

fastening the door and turned in exasperation to see what was amiss. This line of thought was quickly broken off. Shem, it seemed, was not alone! Someone small and wrapped in blankets had reached the door and opened it and fallen very softly just across the sill.

Nor did the bundled figure stir when Shem knelt down beside it and brushed aside the snow. Had someone left a lifeless body here; had somone sought to reach this place and then, falling, died? Shem touched the hands, so cold and still. They reminded him of the curled and tiny claws of a poor dead bird. A breath, a sigh, escaped the narrow lips. He lifted the figure as he rose—even little Annie must weigh more, he thought— and carried it to the bed.

He began to spread his blanket but saw as soon the futility of his intended act: where a body's warmth is gone a covering does no service. Quietly Shem lay down beside the slight and sleeping figure. The only warmth he had to give was his body's own. He sighed and took the stranger in his arms. Then he began to count out loud so he would not fall asleep.

* * *

LETTER FROM SOPHY PERKINS TO HER FATHER

Dear Father,

Expect me in early April. I can resist your pleas no more and shall come when the lakes reopen. I am every where advised against a stage coach journey at this time of year.

I am sorry that it has gone so ill with you. Can our mother not be any help at all? Let the women enjoin her if they can but be sure they are delicate and kind lest she should recoil. Is there not a doctor in Detroit, if not nearer by? If she has a pain she should see one of them.

Here we each have tasks assigned—one to start the kitchen fires, some to make the daily bread, some to peel potatoes. It is very agreeable to know one's responsibilities in this way. Perhaps even Annie might assist with the aid of such a plan.

I have heard from Catherine, my old friend. She is again in New-Hampshire and finds all there are well. I thought you would like to know. Priest Fowle is the exception, as he died. Mistress Shipman's hair is grey, but her life is hard. Asa, who is the second oldest son, has taken up the sailor's life. Portsmouth is his home port. He sailed for England last. Have you heard aught of Catherine's uncle? I sent you some seeds with him. If you know his whereabouts, tell him he should write.

Well, that is all I have to say just now. There is no use telling you of my days at school for they are already numbered. I do not think there will be any money left, but I will endeavor that my fare be paid. Mistress Lyon assures me I will be welcomed back once again when my duties as a daughter are concluded.

I hope this finds you improved in your health and my mother as well. Tell Annie I am proud of her and will bring a new and pretty book to continue her instruction.

Ever your affectionate daughter,
S. Perkins

* * *

XII

An Episode of Indian Justice

SHEM HAD RISEN AFTER A TIME and succeeded in starting the fire. Although it did not warm the room at once, it did drive back the dark. The stranger awakened in some hours, "Bo'jour," she said, "good morning!"

"Good morning," Shem said joyfully, although it still was night.

So, in this first and simplest of exchanges, English was established as the language they would use.

Her name was Mary Goodhue.

Her first employer, many years before, had admired her fair complexion. "I shall call you Goodhue," he had said. "And Mary, that you be pure."

The events of Mary Goodhue's life would be joined to Shem's henceforward. It is therefore necessary to say something of them here.

She was born to Ottawan parents in the reign of George the Third. During the War of American Independence the skirmishes between the English and the French meant more to her than the war itself, for they often involved her people. She had married a youth, an Indian, who was also Ottawan. This hunter came from Canada, which was far beyond the waters of the great blue lake. Thus he was and yet was not kin to her own people. This circumstance may have made a difference. It is hard to tell.

The husband was provident, strong, and kind. The marriage between them prospered. Three small children increased it: two sons and a daughter. In the summers they lived on the Manistee, close by the fields of their village. Then the air was sweet each day with the smell of fruits and berries. In summer the streams were full of fish. When winter came they traveled southward, spending that bitter season where the weather was less severe. This was what they did.

In any season the husband, a clever hunter, could find ample game. So they never wanted and sang many happy songs. In one night all this changed.

A youth well known as troublesome accused the husband wrongly. The husband answered angrily, refusing the false charge. Words soon changed to combat. The fight filled many hours and went on through the night. When daylight brought the husband home, the other youth lay dead.

Hurriedly the village gathered. The husband was a stranger but the youth was of their own. The linkages that bound them all were now disarrayed. That the balance be restored, there must be retribution. Thus, as was required by justice, a death fee was arranged. The hunter must bring many skins to the dead youth's father. So it was argued and so it was done. But so many of the skins? The husband could not pay.

Sad was the murmur that passed among them then. For the husband, though a stranger, was none the less well loved. In failure of the fee, they knew, he must give up his life. After a thoughtful silence the dead youth's father spoke. He who had lost the most of all argued for the other!

Because the husband was so brave, might he not be permitted another hunting trip? If it was intended so, good hunting would be his. In this manner they would know how it was meant to be.

The others heard the wisdom of the plan and proudly the hunter agreed. His return could be expected in the Moon of Flowers on the Feast Day of the Dead.

Winter came, extreme in its cold and storms. Even the oldest persons in the village, with hair as white as snow itself, had not known such a winter in their memory! It locked the great bears in their dens; the martens and the beavers were hidden in the snow. All hearts were with the hunter. No one for a moment doubted that he would return.

When the winter began to be less strong and the snow to shrink within its frozen drifts, the wife commenced a suit of clothes for her welcome gift. Love informed the hands that sewed it. Never were such tiny stitches seen! She used the finest deerskins and only the brightest trim. Daily she told her children of their father, how loyal he was! How brave! But they must not think that he was not afraid! Courage is born of fear, she said. Where no fear exists, she said, there is no need of courage. Her children understood these words. They, too, would be brave.

Now the plants of strawberries appeared! Returning to the village of their summers, the people found the flat-leaved plants in bloom, their tiny flowers centered with droplets of bright gold. Soon there came the heart-shaped berries, with the story, which the people told each spring, of a wife who left her husband but was won again.

The people gathered early on the Feast Day of the Dead. Walking singly, or in silent groups, they took the path from the village to the low hill to the west. At its brow was an oval plain with a young oak at its head. Its leaves were as small as a mouse's ear and absolutely still. In the early morning sky there hung the morning star.

Those facing eastward saw the dawn; the western sky was dark. Slowly the eastern sky turned bright. Then the lovely first rays of the sun touched the topmost branches of the tall-est trees.

Borne as by the light itself, the sound of one voice singing entered the hushed arena, increasing with the light. It was the husband, the hunter; but now the song was Death's.

He did not look to left or right. Finding a place at the center of the meadow, he turned his back to the rising sun, address-ing his whole being to the western sky. There it was his spirit journey lay. He raised his eyes as if in hope of light. The slain youth's brother silently approached. The hunter gave his knife. No one breathed nor swayed nor spoke. The small blade found its mark.

Until his eyes could see no more, so long the hunter stood. Then his legs grew weaker. He fell and quickly died.

Clinging to his body, sobbing, the wife yet held him close.

After a time the slain youth's father spoke. "Rise up, woman," is what he said. "Your husband was a brave man. I think you are also brave. We will give you shelter and care for you with love."

"Gwy-uck," echoed the others, meaning: it is right.

So Mary Goodhue did as he had said. Others taught her sons to hunt. She never took another man nor looked on one with favor. Skilled in the healing ways of herbs, she was well regarded. Her children went their ways. In time she went to the island where the white men had their villages and fort and where the traders lived. She washed their clothes and learned to bake their bread. Here it was that she received her name and, after a time, she became well known for her many acts of healing. Many came to ask her help, even the army surgeon of the Americans! And the Indian agent, Schoolcraft. And Mr. Schoolcraft's lovely, ailing wife, half-Indian, half-English. Acquainted with John Jacob Astor, Mary Goodhue may have been in his employ or else that of his son. How she had loved their pleasant house, elegant with furnishings brought from afar by boat.

One day, time had made her old. Her hair was white and her hands were those of an aging woman. Within herself, not so much had changed. She turned back to her people.

For seven years she lived with them once more in the old and proven ways. For this was also long ago, before the pains began. Now, in the autumn of this year, she knew she could

not travel to the winter lands. She would remain in the summer village, let it happen as it may.

"Gwy-uck," said the others, meaning: it is right.

If too frail to travel, she was yet too strong to die. Day by
day, conserving her stores and her strength, she had watched
the winter deepen. One day, men had come. Why had they
come, she wondered? There was smoke from the cabin, long
unused, and one among them hunted where the others did
not go. If a stone falls in a bucket, the water conceals the
stone. Yet, by the disturbance caused, is its presence known.
She did not need to see the men to know that they were there.

One morning they had gone away. The forest closed in over
them. But no, one yet remained! This one did not hunt so
well. The animals ran freely across the paths he made. She
was worried for his sake. She would wait her time.

The winter advanced another moon. On the night that it
was fully round, a wolf came to her lodge door, seeking hu-
mankind. This was the trail that she had followed. And Shem
knew the rest.

In Michigan, as elsewhere, January's spells of thaw ease a body
on. February, by contrast, is remorseless in its cold. Then
there is neither shadow nor bright sun but only unremitting
gray, the dull recurrence of gray days after darker nights. Together Shem and Mary Goodhue, after she regained her
strength, arranged the cabin's furnishings to accommodate
their needs. The nails Shem saved from the table were now
put to use. He devised a table and benches. Now they might
sit together to eat before the fire.

They stored what remained of the trading goods—blankets, cooking pots, beads, and knives—and placed a mattress near the fire for Mary Goodhue's use. Shem selected as his own the bunk that had the best location. It had been Beaubien's.

On the four remaining bunks they laid their few possessions. These were Shem's axe and writing needs, his blanket, and his gun. Mary Goodhue had her blanket, too, and sent Shem searching in the snow for the sack she had abandoned on the night she came. It contained some baskets filled with meal and her missionary Bible.

After a time she remembered other things that she had left behind. These, she suggested pleasantly, Shem might fetch for her.

"Yes," he said, also pleasant, "when the snow is gone."

"No," she said, "before that. On the snowshoes you can go."

"Those," he said, "are not for the likes of me. They have told me plainly and are proven right."

Mary Goodhue looked at him. "We will see," she said.

At last, one day at midday, the sun broke through the clouds. Shadows appeared on the landscape in a miracle of light. Making a broom of hemlock branches, they swept out the house. Chipmunks caught in hibernation deep beneath the snow awoke, thinking it was spring. They collected several and had meat to eat.

* * *

FROM THE NOTEBOOKS OF SHEM PERKINS: UNDATED ENTRY;
PRESUMED SPRING, 1838.

In this manner we continued our endurance in to the month of March. Under Mary Goodhue's tutelage I at last became proficient with the pair of snow shoes which had been left behind. Before she came I had tried them, but without success. Indeed I had so often and deeply fallen I had thought on more than one occasion that I should never rise. Instead I contrived to shovel out a "yard"—a space before my dwelling which I then kept free of snow. I kept cleared paths to my few traps and placed the woodlot just behind the cabin but at a greater height. I used a deerskin as a sled and, what with dragging it down the slope and up, had a serviceable run.

Now my circumstance was changed. If I had, in Mary Goodhue, one who could provide me with instruction, it was her very presence that increased my need. The arithmetic was simple: on one side, one to teach me; on the other, one to feed. . . .

We began not with the snow shoes but removal of my boots. From the outset she was certain that they helped me not at all. Indeed, she believed they were the cause of my frustrated efforts to use the shoes before. Also, she thought to caution me that I must learn, with the snow shoes, to throw each heel out wide.

I, to throw my heels out wide? I, who counted it a mercy to walk a simple step?

"Can is not the question," she replied. "You will do it. It must be."

So, at her insistence, I exchanged my boots and stockings for mocassins and neips. Awkward, embarrassed, and ashamed, I learned to cross the cabin floor and then I traversed the yard. We cut a sturdy walking stick, which I found to help me very much. And then we came round to the snow shoes, which had been the point.

Day by day I practiced and improved. Some days I did *not* improve, and often the bindings cut my feet so badly that they bled. She felt that I must make my first trips soon, before thaw spoilt the snow. Once as she bathed my painful feet she began to speak of the medicines which were at her lodge. These, she felt, would help me. It was good that I could fetch them soon. They would help me very much, and not solely in the injuries I had now acquired.

All the time she had had this in her mind!

There came a day at the end of March when the snow seemed to be right. As the river which ran before my door nourished the fields of her village, I only had to follow the frozen river's course. This had been the path the wolf had taken. It would not be too far.

I reached the place quite comfortable, in fact, and collected the sacks which she'd described and some half-full of meal. I saw that she'd been well provided. Not all of those who left her there had thought that she would die! However, the returning trip was much more difficult. I was tired by my efforts and now carried a full pack. I had thought to stop and rest, but was impatient to return and tell of my achievement. It was joy as well that bore me on: I, the Fiddler's crippled son, had walked across the snow alone and fallen not, nor faltered.

That night she gave me warming broths and rubbed my swollen, aching legs with a concoction she had brewed of the bark and roots I'd brought. Sleep was deep and welcome. Once I woke to feed the fire and once I heard the wolf. Mary Goodhue—did she wake or sleep?—sighed once and slept on.

In the morning I was greatly healed. I used the snow shoes frequently thereafter, and what came as a consequence is yet another story.

* * *

XIII

A Dull Task Is Diverted

IN THE WOODS the hepatica leafed; there, too, the trillium bloomed. The sun was warm where it struck the forest floor and warmer still where it came to rest before Fiddler Perkins' house.

Sophy stood there, stretching like a cat. When she'd come, a few short weeks before, everything was closed against the cold, as she, herself, was closed against the place, not having wished to come. Now it was almost pretty. The little village, raw and new, was gentled by the sun.

She caught the sound of distant voices, her father's and Uncle Jack's. The men had gone out early in the day to resume the work of clearing. It was nice, she thought, to have them near at hand. By the very sounds of their axes and their saws one could know how the work progressed and slowed, when they, too, paused to rest.

She knew she ought to go inside but could not bear to do so. In the dark interior of the house her mother spent her days. When Sophy came she'd tried to talk with her but she soon gave up the effort, just as the others had. There was nothing her mother wanted; she was not in pain. "It's just"—the deep eyes lifted—"it's just—." She didn't know.

When Annie went to her she'd say, "Go find your sister, Sophy" or "You ask Sophy now." Once, when she made some pudding and it scorched, she had cried just like a child.

Today when Sophy made the weekly bread, kneading it till her shoulders ached, her mother had watched her dully, not offering to help. The loaves lay close together now, pale, and plumply rising under a linen cloth.

That was what she ought to do: go in and bake the bread. Sophy thought that, when the bread was baked, she'd carry a loaf to Uncle Jack's to wait on his coming home. He had been so good to them these weeks! A loaf of bread was small in the way of thanks but surely the thing to do. She would not stay to speak with him, just put the loaf on the table. He would find it in good time.

This decided to her satisfaction, her mind began to run more briskly in its accustomed manner. So, while the bread was in the oven, she would write the letter that was now long overdue.

* * *

FROM SOPHIA PERKINS TO CATHERINE HALL

Millfield, Michigan
April 4, 1838

Dearest Catherine,

So much new assails me here I scarcely can begin! Having waited till the roads were free of ice I had the pleasure of journeying by every modern means! By stage at first, and then canal, I made my way conveniently as far as Buffalo. I then embarked upon a steamer by which I crossed Lake Erie. From Detroit the rail road brought me—with hardly a stop or mishap—to a handy distance from my parents' home.

Here all are well except my mother, on whose account I came. My hopes for a swift return are dashed. I see no improvement. Her present state, so low in mind, is dismaying to us all. I had very much to do to put the house to rights.

The settlement here is quite advanced—more than I had expected! There are nearly six hundred in residence, and more arriving every day by wagon, stage, and rail. We expect to have a proper depot soon. We have one street with its side walk nicely laid, a great boon in mud season! Mostly the houses are of frame & very pleasant size, two storeys, with windows front and back.

Of my brother there is yet no word. It is nearly seven months now and hard to keep up hope. He had not taken all his clothes nor had he left a message here nor sent a letter since. The only person with whom he seems to have had a friendship is the daughter of the homesteader who employed him briefly.

I am far too busy to think about myself! Miss Lyons' school seems but a dream—was it only weeks ago I trod those dear, beloved halls? I do try not to dwell on this and persevere to read each day to keep my spirits up. I was so happy in that place and for so short a while.

If you hold me in your heart, you will write and tell me how you are. I thirst for every word of you. As you know, I am, as ever, your true and loving friend.

Sophia Perkins

I expect you will have heard by now from your father's brother.
I saw him following my arrival and conveyed your message of
concern that he had not written. He is doing nicely here. I
think he is well liked.

S.P.

* * *

When Sophy took her bread around, carrying it the mile or
two, nicely covered, fragrant, warm, the little dwelling in the
woods was not unoccupied. Wearing just his farmer's smock,
bare legs fully visible, there sat Uncle Jack! His trousers, which
he was mending, were spread across his lap. At least he did
not laugh at her—she was sure her cheeks were flaming red—
and the latchstring *had* been out!

"I'm sorry," he said easily, "that I can't get up to welcome
you. But come on in and rest. You sit there." He pointed to a
keg. And Sophy, too embarrassed to object, silently obeyed.

Hands crossed primly in her lap, she stared at him in silence. He stitched away contentedly, pulling his thread to
arm's length, then plunging the needle in. Uncle Jack seemed
quite at ease; if anything, amused. Did he not know, she wondered, that a shorter sewing thread would serve him so much
better?

"Pretty morning," she observed. She'd never seen a man
who sewed before! Perhaps they all preferred it so? He looked
so very satisfied, she would not offer help.

How could she make a suitable excuse and take an early
leave? What about the bread she'd brought? She couldn't

pretend it was not there but now felt very awkward about her intended gift.

"Look the other way," he said. And then again, "All's well."

When Sophy at last vouchsafed a look, he was fully clothed.

"Got to tidy up," he said, reaching for a broom. He implied by his manner that it was quite the common thing to have one's mending thus observed and company while one swept.

He plied his broom with cheerful vigor. Sophy watched him, fascinated. You would think she'd never seen a floor get swept before!

"Lift your feet," he commanded. "Higher," he said and gestured with his hand until it was enough. Then he swept beneath her feet and released her with a bow.

Sweeping done and rush broom pegged, he began to rearrange the furnishings in the room. A chair reappeared from brief storage in the loft; a table was drawn from a corner and given a central place. She realized that she'd come on him in the midst of a general cleaning.

As if to confirm her still unspoken thought, he volunteered offhandedly, "Split the things while sweeping! A good thing I had thread!"

She nodded, too discomfited to speak, but with friendly interest.

"I'm sorry you found it awkward," he went on. "You couldn't have known, of course."

"I thought," she said, "I heard you in the woods, and my father, too. I only meant to leave the bread—had I known that you were here—"

"You'd not have come," he finished. "It's my good fortune,

your mistake; else I might have missed you! Why, just this very day I said, 'Jack, you've got to clean this place! Supposing someone thinks to call; you wouldn't want it said in town that a man who's single cannot keep a house.' "

He glanced at her and caught the faintest smile. Encouraged, he continued. "It's not the worst thing in the world, living as I do. Say, once I courted with a girl whose father was hard of hearing. So when it came to ask her hand, I went to speak with him alone and found him in the barn. The old man put his pitchfork by, and I said, very plainly, 'Sir, I want to marry with your daughter.'

" 'You want to borrow my halter? Oh, I would lend it to you, Jack, but happens my son is using it just now, and he's down to the mill.'

" 'Sir,' I said, to make a new attack, 'I've got five hundred pounds of money, neither more nor less.'

" 'Five hundred pounds of *honey*, Jack? Now what'd you want with that?'

" 'Sir,' I shouted, desperate for sure, *'I've got gold!'*

" 'Well, so have I,' says he to me, 'and I'll tell you, Jack, it's the worst darn cold that I ever had!' "

The margin of mannerly self-restraint is fixed. Sophy's had been reached. Following his story closely, discovering how neatly she'd been tricked, she could not help but laugh.

"That's better," he said lightly. And then they talked of many pleasant things, having much in common.

She was tardy getting back; the afternooon was waning. Never mind, she told herself, as she started preparations for the evening meal. She had not had so good a time since she left Miss Lyons'. The worst darn cold I ever had, she repeated to herself. Her mother, looking up just then, caught her daughter smiling.

Within the space of the next few weeks, visits were exchanged. Sometimes he would come to call just like a proper suitor. Sometimes she would find a small excuse to visit at the Ellsworths', their new house being situated just before his cabin.

Almost, it seemed, despite herself, Lydia Perkins became aware of her daughter's friendship with the bachelor, Uncle Jack. It drew her back to her own courting days when she was young and pretty: how grand Tom had looked to her—handsome, and more cheerful than her other swains; how, right in the middle of a square, all eyes upon his glancing bow, he'd hand the fiddle on midtune and snap her up to dance!

> We're all a-marching to Quebec;
>   The drums are loudly beating,
> The Americans have won the day,
>   And the British are retreating;
>
> The wars are o'er, and we'll turn back
>   To the place from whence we started;
> So open the ring and choose a couple in
>   To relieve the brokenhearted.

He would always play "We're Marching to Quebec" because she liked it best. Two by two they'd promenade—how d'you do and how d'you do—and Tom would hold her nice and close with his strong young arm about her. At last a large ring would be formed. Then they'd circle on, still singing, till someone indeed would open up the ring and choose another partner. But not her and Tom.

Oh, it all came back to her. But nothing had relieved their hearts the night that Shem was born to them and they had cried together.

XIV

A Coin of French Design

THE SUCCESS OF SHEM'S FIRST VENTURE encouraged his return. Over the succeeding weeks he fetched from Mary Goodhue's lodge baskets whose contents she did not reveal and some bundles of excellent furs. Many of these reflected her own skills, for among her people a woman was expected to be independent in the use of traps and snares. Obedient to her clear instructions concerning them, their concealment and situation, he set new traps at greater ranges and enjoyed renewed success. In the nights, secure within the cabin, he worked to improve and repair his traps, while Mary Goodhue stitched fur strips together that they might have new blankets. These were the times of Mary Goodhue's stories. A long life. Many stories.

A stand of maples suggested to them both that they tap them and make syrup. Shem worked hard to improvise the pegs, and finding his buckets full of sap filled him with new pride. The cabin's air was steamy as Mary Goodhue boiled the liquid till its flavor deepened. After the winter diet, the pure sweet taste was a pleasure beyond compare. They laughed as they licked their fingers to savor every drop.

Returning through the woods one day with a bucket full of sap, Shem came upon a line of tracks that were not his own. They seemed to wander with the slope and did not impose upon its surface a clear and vigorous course. What to make of them? He saw that the steps were smaller than his own and ragged in their placement. One who was moving strongly would not leave such a trail.

Shem placed his bucket carefully and followed the other's trail. Two of his steps, he noted with surprise, matched the other's three. He came to a ridge and crossed it. On the lee side, motionless, a man lay in the cold. The man was large of frame, and broad. It was only with the greatest effort that Shem at last succeeded in turning him from his prone position. The still face that looked up at him was that of Bad Pierre.

* * *

FROM THE NOTEBOOKS, EXCERPT ONLY:

My immediate thought was for the other men: Beaubien, and Good Pierre, and Zozep, most of all. He it was who, over time, had engendered my affection by his constant care. Had they after all returned? Where might they be this moment? There was no indication they were any where about.

However curious I was, my questions would have to wait. I saw that the man's condition was very low and my efforts failed to rouse him. Whatever one's feelings toward a man, one does not wish him such an end to his life on earth. Mary Goodhue would know what to do. We must reach the cabin.

Although I then redoubled my attempts to awaken him to consciousness, he remained insensate of my activity. I could not stay beyond the daylight hours, and presently I concluded that whatever help I had to offer I must offer here.

Accordingly I cleared the snow away and heaped it as I did so, forming a wall or barricade against the freezing wind. I found his blanket and laid it over him. After a moment's hesitation I doubled it with mine.

I took from my pocket some food for when he woke: dried meat and meal cake. I made a little prayer in my mind, trying to think of the good in him, tho' I could not think of much. Satisfied that my duties were fulfilled, I then allowed myself to do what I had dreamed repeatedly since I had seen him last.

* * *

Every woodsman in those days carried about his person a small pouch made of leather. In this he carried items he must keep dry or those of special value. Often the pouch, or pocket as it was called, was carried against the body, underneath the shirt.

Shem was certain that the man who lay there now carried something in his pouch that should not be there. Eagerly he withdrew the little sack and undid the ties. There, as he'd expected, was the gold coin of French design, a coin that might have fallen from a Frenchman's pack, or an Indian's, on a New Hampshire hillside many years before.

Shem's own narrative now concludes, "I followed my own trail going back and allowed myself a smile. Perhaps I had done the reprobate a favor in relieving him of the evidence of one earthly sin."

In one of those surprising shifts of weather for which the state is famous, the air next day seemed springlike and the sun was bright. Shem was all for returning to the place where Bad Pierre had lain. But Mary Goodhue was adamant in her opposition. The fellow would not welcome him, she said. Having found the French coin gone, he would know who found him there and Shem, despite his kindness, would receive no thanks.

But supposing he had died? That was Shem's concern. Even such a one as this deserved a burial. Here again Mary Goodhue was notably unimpressed. She did not think that a dead Pierre would appreciate Shem's efforts more than the same man, live. Her final and closing argument concerned the snow's condition: it would be heavier, with the thaw, and difficult to travel.

Shem spent the day at writing, excluding her thereby. Then, throughout the next two days, there was more new snow. On the fourth day Shem put on his snow shoes, determined to set out. Although the skies still threatened snow he must attend his traps. As he left, neither he nor Mary Goodhue mentioned Bad Pierre although it was clear to both of them that he was on Shem's mind.

Shem became very frightened as he made his approach. This was the man who was terrible in his strength and easily provoked. Suppose he *had* survived these days and now awaited Shem? Shem had left the French coin at the cabin, reasoning silently that what he did not have he also could not yield. He came over the final slope.

Relief and disappointment mingled as Shem saw that the drifted snow was trampled and Bad Pierre was gone. He thought how he might have made a brilliant rescue or waged a valiant fight! Neither was to be. Yet as he turned and started home, he felt supremely happy. It was as if Bad Pierre had taken the badness when he left. It was as if the French coin's luck was back with Shem once more.

Having endured both trespass and dispute, Shem and Mary Goodhue now began to speak of things they'd hitherto left unspoken: of her life, so beautiful and good, when she was a girl. How she'd had many suitors and a father who was brave. She was her father's favorite daughter. He had taught her many things. When even now she walked on the paths of the forest, it seemed that he was near. From her mother she had learned of herbs, cures, and concoctions. Her mother had the gift of curing. People came to her for help. She was very wise.

Shem told how he could not go to school when the path was icy and he was still small. His mother taught him how to read and also how to write. She would take his hand in hers to guide him through the letters. It sometimes smelled of flour and the bread she had just made.

More and more they lived in story, and as they told the stories back and forth, the storied whole became the place where both of them might dwell. It was a quiet, strange time in their lives, mingling past and present. Because now her strength was ebbing, and both knew it was so.

In her village, Mary Goodhue said, none of the youths who

lived there were pleasing to her eye. As one repelled her by his boastful ways, another caused impatience by seeming to her too shy. She did not like the cut of this one's jaw. Another's teeth were crooked. Then from Canada came the one she wed with joyous heart!

Oh, they had been happy in those times! The grass was not disturbed beneath their feet, so lightly did they tread. When her babies came to her, it was lovely in each season. Proud of them, their father was, and cradled each one gently for all he was so strong. As she told these things to Shem, she seemed once more the young and happy wife who turns to greet her husband. Then the illusion vanished and she was old once more.

There was one more thing Shem knew he had to tell, yet he did not wish to do so. He remembered, he said slowly, standing on a bridge. The river roiled beneath it. He paused, reluctant to go on. This was about his brother and how his brother died.

Shem had loved—had *admired* him so much, more than all the others. ("Keep it, Shemmy! It's yours for luck." Oh, he would! He would!) Shem had gone with his father on an errand. Where they'd gone, he did not know; possibly the mill. He had shared the saddle and, at six, delightedly had helped to rein the horse. Their business was not completed when the sun was suddenly erased by a bank of thunder clouds.

Knowing his wife's long terror of such storms, the Fiddler cut short his errand. The horse was young and skittish in the quickly breaking storm. They had to fight their way across, leading the horse—too frightened to obey—while the rain kept on in torrents. Beneath the bridge were tree roots sweeping by, a barrel, and some planking. Shem could not keep his footing in the driving rain. His father tried to carry him and still lead the horse.

Then a bright red shirt whirled by.

"Oh, my God, Shem! *Don't look down!*"

And leaving Shem, tossing the reins aside, his father raced across the bridge, turning once as he reached the other side: *"Go home, Shem."*

Numbly Shem obeyed. It took so long to reach his house, but he did hold to the horse. His mother met him at the door. Sophy, too, her hair about her face. There were sad-faced men with his father, in the back, and his brother looked so queer, so still, on the front-room bed. Shem knew before he went to him that the flood had killed him and that was why he died.

Mary Goodhue's eyes were wet when Shem at last fell silent.

"Long ago," she said quietly, "heaven and earth were one. This is our way of saying that earth and heaven were the same; life here was that sweet. The stem of a great vine joined earth to heaven. The spirits traveled on that vine, going back and forth. Only the spirits used that vine; to men it was forbidden.

"Then, just once, a young boy disobeyed. He climbed so high he nearly disappeared! His mother was so afraid! Meaning to climb up after him, she put one foot upon the vine— and down it came upon her. Great was the sound when it fell.

"The Great Spirit was angry at all that disobedience. He made it that they would not live forever, made pain and death and sickness to come among them then. The earth, still fair, seemed not so beautiful. The people were sad and troubled, not knowing what to do.

"At last the Great Spirit took pity. He came among them kindly. He said, 'You went against the purpose of that vine; therefore you were punished. Learn the use of all that grows, of every thing that happens.' "

Shem could make no sense of this. He felt she had not understood the story he had told her with its painful memories. "I was telling you," he said, "about my brother, that was Luke, and how he came to die."

"Exactly so," she answered. "And *I* am telling you how it was the medicine lodge began."

This last confused Shem utterly. Annoyed and disappointed, he got up from his place.

Nor did it help his outlook any that when he visited his traps he missed his footing and fell forward into some new sprung nettles. They stung his hands, instinctively outflung, and Mary Goodhue, seeing them, knew instantly what had happened. She sighed, as she studied his set, unhappy face. He still had so much to learn. They had so little time.

Yet she waited till the hands were healed before she tried to speak with him again of more than routine matters.

"Shem," she said then, "listen to me now. Think that when the nettles start to grow that is also when their leaves make a healing tea." She saw he did not understand. "They sting, Shem, but they also heal. Think what I have told you. I can say no more."

XV

Hands Outstretched
and Hopeful

MILLFIELD HAD, IN APRIL, much to talk about. The railroad had begun its operation. Tracks to extend its westward thrust were even now under way. Meanwhile, those who'd laid the tracks, the builders and the laborers, sought food and recreation in the town itself. Even to provide accommodation pressed the town to limits. On the other hand, there were clear financial gains. So if some complained, there were others who were pleased with all they had achieved.

On a clear, warm day such as early spring bestows, Alice Howe, the printer's wife, had washed her bed sheets well. Then she had spread them out to dry as was the common custom. While she was absent from the house, a vandalous and bold attack had ruined the sheets completely. Cut, they were, with knife blades that slashed them through and through.

Her wedding sheets! Her wedding dowry sheets! One could not hope to have such sheets again, each being made of finest cloth and hemmed with special care. They were softened now with years of steady use, but still firm and strong.

The destruction of Alice Howe's good sheets was not the first example of local rowdyism. Gates had been sprung and windows marked. Each time, in *The Courier*, there were editorials followed by angry letters. If the rowdies read the newspaper, they were not impressed.

Their mischief, pranks, and nuisances went on. Be it said that in the latest incident, the protest was quite mild. Perhaps there were some in Millfield who yet felt that their atheistic printer had gotten his comeuppance in this act against his wife. Indeed, the story of the sheets was told for years thereafter. In time it achieved a humorous patina, one of the lustier episodes of a small town's early days.

But the story had a second part, much less widely known. When Mrs. Perkins learned of what had happened, she felt that there was something she must do if only she remembered. Hours later, sitting in her chair, she called out for Sophy. But it hadn't to do with Sophy and she didn't want her there.

Nor Annie, she realized.

Once there were sons and daughters. Now there were no sons. Luke had died, but where was Shem? Did it have to do with Shem? He was there and then was not and no one knew what happened as no one saw him go.

Except that one *had* seen him go and had, at length, come forward. He was not a godly man, but goodly all the same. Goodly, godly; godly, goodly. They were not so far apart. Now they said his wife's sheets were destroyed. They thought she did not know of this, but she did, she did!

And she had far too many sheets because of those who once were here but were here no more.

"Sophy?" she called out. She had fixed on what she meant to do, if Sophy would assist.

So Sophy helped her find two sheets with edges good and nicely turned—you needn't be ashamed of them—and neither one was darned. She would take them to the printer's wife. Take them there herself. It was the least that she could do. Debts were canceled if repaid. Hers was gratitude.

For the first time in how many weeks she left the house unescorted and made a proper call. The printer's wife was nearly overcome and begged her guest to stay. No, said Mrs. Perkins firmly, that she could not do. She only wanted Mrs. Howe to know she certainly was sorry about those ruined sheets.

* * *

FROM ASA SHIPMAN TO CATHERINE HALL (IN BOSTON).
FRAGMENT ONLY:

. . . England is very beautiful just now. They have got a new queen, very young, called Victoria. I have seen her carriage it is gold and drawn by finer horses than you could wish to see. If I get passage back to Portsmouth I have hopes of seeing you before the summer's out.

* * *

FROM CATHERINE HALL TO SOPHY PERKINS. FRAGMENT ONLY:

. . . M. has lent me Mr. Hawthorne's book which he calls *Twice-Told Tales*. This is because some of them have already appeared in print. I think that very clever and surely you agree!

M. says I need not hurry the book's return, he estimates that the book will be enhanced by its stay with me! Is he not a flatterer? I . . .

* * *

Tell me not of Mr. Hawthorne's book. *Who is M.?*

* * *

As someone's trials are comforted, another's may begin. Soon, on a pleasant afternoon, with no one expecting trouble of any sort, the rowdies reappeared. This time, though, they teased the mayor's own daughter, a pretty little thing.

The town had had enough of them, of protest and reproach! What they did not do for the printer's wife was quickly enacted now. Scarcely had the girl's tears dried when seven prominent citizens met in a room behind the tavern. Objective: swift revenge. Three of the men were good friends of the mayor's. They named themselves the Intrepidites and promptly launched a course of actions conspicuous and loud. Some were in retaliation and some less purposeful. In boisterousness the Intrepidites fully matched the vandals they meant to oppose.

No one was ever brought to justice, no one was ever named. Within a year of the Intrepidites' formation the problem had abated; then it disappeared. Millfield was more than grateful that all was calm once more. Some credited the Intrepidites; others connected the situation—first its emergence and then its decline—with the scores of laborers who brought the railroad through.

One year more and the railroad was on its way. Soon it would reach Jackson, to the west, and there were some who spoke of plans to run the thing up north. It was all a part of their ambitious plan to improve the state.

* * *

FROM A LETTER FROM JOHN (JACK) HALL TO SOPHIA PERKINS:

Cincinatti, Ohio
Saturday, May 12, 1838

My very dearest Sophy,

I surprise myself with thoughts of you, or rather you surprise me as ever in my thoughts! Do I behold a new delight? I must fix it in my mind to tell you of it later! Do I find myself perplexed? I need only ask myself: what would Sophy say?

. . . My business here is nearly done. I shall soon make preparation for the journey homeward. I think of you so much.

* * *

FIRST PAGE ONLY OF LETTER SENT BY SOPHIA PERKINS TO
CATHERINE HALL:

Millfield, Michigan
Wednesday, May 9

Dearest Catherine,

The reasons for which I came are done: my mother's health is much restored tho' not, I think, through offices of mine; and my father has employment. He is the station master with Michigan Central Rail Road and the post becomes him well.

It is sweet to think I may return to my studies soon. However, I do not wish to travel unless the roads are healed somewhat of their annual affliction with the springtime mud. Also, I believe, I am become quite fond of your Uncle Jack.

After our first and comical encounter we saw each other more. He has taught me very much; I now call him John. One day, in the early Spring, he led me to a hidden place where the white hepatica carpeted the woods. It was rare and peaceful there, and when we had regained the house he kissed me, on the lips.

At present he is gone—Port Lawrence—and perhaps beyond. You will understand, dear friend, that I am rather less in haste to conclude my visit than might have been the case.

We are becoming quite civilized here! The next town to the west of us keeps two doctors busy and sustains a grocery store! Recently they commenced the publication of a weekly newspaper. There is less building and more planting now; they intend to convert the saw mill to a flour mill. I must tell John of this. Two banks have applied for charter, all of this appearing to reflect the encouraging influence of the railroad here. Generally, throughout the state, conditions are less hopeful. . . .

* * *

FROM THE NOTEBOOKS (1836-1838) OF JOHN HALL:

The truth is that there *is* no truth, only that one quiddity we call the universe. Toward its reality we advance, our hands outstretched and hopeful, blueberries in our pails.

August 16, 1836

Always there is the one choice to be made: which road to take? which duty to accept? which item, amidst a store's displays, to purchase as our own? The paths of the past parts of our lives are strewn with things not chosen. One believes, nay, one is *taught,* that choice provides fulfillment of desire. In truth, however, relinquishment and loss enter in to the bargain every single time. Loss looks over the shoulders of fair choice. For every thing one chooses, some thing is left behind.

September 10, 1837

Six be the principal attitudes of mind: to love, to hate, to ask, to learn, to hold, and to let go.

(undated)

* * *

John Hall, when he put his case, was nothing if not fair. He reviewed with Sophy much she already knew and some that she hadn't considered. He did not press her answer and he dwelt on the harder parts.

"It is your choice," he said to her at last. "You must know that clearly."

"Love is not something you choose about," she said. "There is every reason, save one, for me to go. And for *that one* I will stay."

Then she turned away from him because she hoped he would not see the tears that filled her eyes. There was so much she was giving up. The thought of it, in that moment, was terrible to bear.

XVI

He Who Makes Me Happy

A SOUND HE HAD NEVER HEARD BEFORE woke Shem in the night. Mary Goodhue, wide awake, laughed at him for springing up, gun gripped in his hand.

"Shem!" she said. "The ice is breaking up! Soon you can go home."

"Home?" he repeated. "But I am at home."

"No," she said. "Go to sleep."

Next morning, when he stepped outside, each tree seemed distinct against the sky, which was blue and clear. He stood there with the water buckets, which he filled first thing each day, wondering what seemed different. It was the water moving in the lake, having been still all winter. And Shem, who never ran before, was plunging down the hillside in great uneven leaps.

As he stood beside the river he looked back up at the slope. In the night had a rabbit run across? Was other small game stirring? If so, he must check his traps; if not, they might wait. But all that he saw of interest was the trail of his downhill

flight. He would tell Mary Goodhue; she would be so surprised!

Looking toward the cabin now, he missed the expected curl
of smoke from its stubby chimney. That was what they did
each day: he went out to fetch the water, she began the fire.
Oh, but he would tease her for lying abed so late!

Throwing wide the cabin door, "Gwy-uck!" he called. "Bo'
jour! Good morning!" It was a little joke with them, recalling
their first day.

When there was no answer to his greeting, he drew aside
the sacking they had hung beside her bed. A terrible trans-
formation had happened in the night. An old, old woman lay
there now—one whose life was ending.

The closed eyes opened, Mary Goodhue's eyes; but they
seemed not to know him for they searched his face. As if in
sorrow the small lids closed, leaving him alone.

"Good morning," Shem called after her. "Good morning!
Oh, *good morning!*"

Awakened by his anguished shouting, Mary Goodhue
turned to him as if intending speech.

"Shem," she managed, short of breath, "medicine. The
pain." He knelt and took her hands in his. Something was taking her breath away. It frightened him. He waited.

Mary Goodhue's head had cleared. "Shem," she said, "the
pain is back. It is as I told you. *Get the medicine bag.*"

Now he knew what it was she had in mind. Not real medicine, not like home. Not neat powders, stoppered in small
bottles made of deep-blue glass. She was asking for the bits of

bark, the roots and leaves she carried with her always in the leather pocket tied about her waist.

From underneath her bed he fetched it and opened it out wide.

"This," she said, "and this, and this," sorting it with her fingers. "After the water is hotted, then you put it in."

But first he must restart the fire. Careful! If you hurry, it will only put it out.

The kettle, it is not too full. Good, it will heat the faster. He saw that now she watched him but was only half awake. He was so afraid that she would fall asleep. He was so afraid.

In his first weeks at the cabin, Shem had often considered that he well might die. Now again he lived with thoughts of death. But this time it was certain, and this time not his own. Although some days the pain was less severe, Mary Goodhue had not long to live. Both knew this was so.

* * *

FROM THE NOTEBOOKS OF SHEM PERKINS:

April 24, 1838   Mary Goodhue believes that I should go, leaving her to meet her death alone as she is not afraid. She argues that I would be home in time to help with planting. I am most opposed to this and have told her so. Also, there are the trading goods left by Beaubien. I must report to Mr. Prentice their amount and whereabouts.

April 25, 1838   Mary Goodhue again not well, having suffered severely during this past night. Today spoke of my family, how she imagines each of them to look. What would be this cooking stove? What is a railroad *carriage?*

April 27, 1838   Clearing, after last night's storm. Thunder very heavy for this time of year. We are agreed that I shall not depart till her spirit starts its journey or her people come. At such time I will travel to Detroit, to give account of all that has transpired, and then I will go home. It is my wish to travel by canoe. Began to plan that journey, what will be required.

April 28, 1838   Clear and warm. All day without pain. Recommenced my instruction in the Indian speech.

April 29, 1838   Cooler and windy. Mary Goodhue instructed me concerning her death and burial. I have promised faithfully to do all that she asks.

* * *

Because he would be traveling alone through regions used by Indians, it was important that Shem be fluent in the Ottawan language, its phrases and their use. Again and again they practiced.

"Where do you dwell?"

"I dwell in the place of mill fields, where my people are."

"Is it at a distance?"

"I will go there by canoe."

They had many conversations, carefully constructing them around the words Shem knew.

"Are you well?" she asked him once.

"I am thirsty," he replied, collapsing her with laughter.

On and on their lessons surged, rehearsing the language,

the customs, the common courtesies. Always walk before a woman. Eat until the bowl is drained. Never call attention to yourself or to your achievements. Most of all, the words.

"Who was brave?"

"Pontiac and Tecumseh were both very brave."

"That was good, Shem. Tell me, what is that?"

"It is a handsome knife."

"Tell me, what has happened?"

"I was running when I fell."

Having recognized that she would die and established also what he needs must do, Shem felt released from fear. Something that verged on humor now infused his attitude. Before, he'd feared that the very least exertion might worsen her condition. Convinced now that it did not matter, he found himself quite reckless. He acquiesced without dispute in the things she asked of him. They went once more to see the lake, blue now in its beauty. They ate as often as they pleased, or, if they were out all day, might not eat except the fruits she found along the way. As merrily as conspirators intent on some nefarious plan, they occupied their days.

Often, and in great detail, they went over and revised Shem's plans for his journey. Overland, the distance to Detroit was several hundred miles. To walk this would be difficult, especially for Shem. On the other hand, with a bark canoe, there would be portages. She had heard men tell of them; only one of them was long. He would be all right.

But how might he acquire a canoe? He had no money of his own and the stores of goods, not plentiful, were strictly Beaubien's.

Mary Goodhue paused in thought. "In my lodge, Shem, there are yet fine furs. You will go and fetch them. It is my wish that they be yours, and with them, your canoe." Speaking slowly, she went on, "Also find a packet wrapped in blue. Bring that here as well."

Shem nodded. He would do this. In the morning he would go.

The village was not so very far as Shem had thought at first. Or perhaps it was that he'd become accustomed to the distance and could pace himself. He found the things she'd asked for and lifted them to his back. On his portages he'd have much to carry. He would practice now!

Shem had almost turned to go when, from the encircling brush, a wolf emerged, inquired of the air, and slowly crossed the field.

Leaving the village, Shem discerned a path that the snow had hidden when he'd been there before. Many persons passing there had firmed the earth so often that there grass would not grow. The path led westward from the village, climbing through the forest to an oval plain. The plain was ringed around with trees. Shem had reached, he knew with certainty, the place where, many springs ago, justice unrelenting had claimed a brave man's life.

Struck by the beauty of the place, Shem paused at the margin of the field so perfect in its proportion that it seemed it had been planned. He thought of all that brought him here and how much lay ahead. Balanced at the center of his life, he was reverent, and calm.

* * *

Some days later Shem and Mary Goodhue had taken their benches out of doors to relish the warming sun. A sound like that of light rain falling issued from the forest although the day was bright. Mary Goodhue turned.

"So," she said, "the pine tree weeps anew! She weeps too easily, I think. Each of us knows sorrow, but not all display their tears." Minutes passed. She drifted in the past. How long had it been, Shem wondered. And still all lines of thought ran there, as a stream will make its way to the mother water. No, he thought, that is not right. A stream runs ever *from* its source. He must remember that.

"Shem," she asked, "do you remember what it means: *main-wain-dumeid?*"

"He who makes me happy," Shem replied, wondering at her purpose in asking this question now.

"Shem," she said, "it has come on me that you and he are brothers; brothers of the heart. In your manhood he will live. By his courage, wisdom, strength, yours will be increased."

It was a strange equation, but it balanced in his mind.

"Yes," he told her softly. "I am proud to be his kin."

"Shem," she said, "the packet wrapped in blue. You will know when it is to be yours. More I cannot say."

Time went by. One minute? Five?

"So," she said and signaled with her hand, as she did in giving lessons. "So," she said, "what have you there?"

"A handsome knife," Shem answered. "And Pontiac and Tecumseh were very, very brave."

Then there was only time. Time, having lost all sense of

flow, became instead an oceanic space. There might events await each other, their influence the tide that rolls between the unseen shores. Time was space, so luminous and vast, in which to lie so quietly these last days of a life.

XVII

Not Fearing Any Death

As Mary Goodhue taught Shem of her people, she had stressed the principles and precepts that unified their lives. Often she had reminded him that it was prohibited to mimic or to ridicule the lame, the crippled, and the deformed. Those, it was said, who disobeyed would be swiftly punished.

Knowing this, Shem knew he would be safe, that wherever he went in that wilderness, no Ottawan would lay hand on him or cause him any mischief on account of his bad leg. Also, through Mary Goodhue's teaching, he knew the words of friendship, of commerce and inquiry. Not only Ottawan did he know, but also those Chippewan variants that she thought that he might need. He could thus explain his mission and with the furs—so luxuriant, so fine—he could trade for equipment and provisions, as much as he might need.

He imagined he'd be home midsummer. Would Margaret remember him? That was not the question. Would she have forgiven him? Or would she be angry at him still for the way he'd disappeared? Would she have made other friends—

friends who partnered her at dances, making her proud before the rest when they circled the hall together?

So Shem's mind ran on ahead while all the while he sat and
waited, close by Mary Goodhue's bed, quiet and attentive. It
was now a full six weeks since the illness struck.

Seeing that she was growing very weak, he brought her
warm, nutritious broths, but nothing seemed to help. Then
it was her story came to mind, and he remembered what she'd
said of the nettle's leaves. He found some readily enough, it
being in the proper season, and, steeping them in heated
water, brought her tea to drink.

She smiled and took it gratefully.

"There is a use," she whispered, too tired to go on.

"Yes," Shem said, "a use for all that happens, for every
thing that grows."

"I thought," she said, "I thought you had not heard."

"Hush, now," he said soothingly. "I was cross that day."

Thou shalt be brave and not fear any death. So Mary Goodhue
had been taught and she did not fear her death. Firmly she
told Shem what to do when her life began to fail.

One day she turned her face to him. "Shem?" she said. "Be
sure that you remember. Brothers. Of the heart." Then, laps-
ing into Ottawan, and sleep, *"Main-wain-dumeid."*

It was two days after this that Mary Goodhue died. The
cabin door was open to the air, and it seemed that the earth,
in its turning, had taken her into its own.

When it began to happen as she said, Shem had washed
and dressed her and raised her up in bed. Correctly, she was

facing toward the west when the breath of life departed. So, in the way of her people, she had wished to die. Shem hoped that in her final dream her husband, healed, had met her with gifts and tender words. Yes, thought Shem, with brimming eyes, they would be united now where the great drum beats for dancing and the spirits of the good may be found together.

He attended to the burial and covered the grave with branches.

"Great good author of life," he read from the paper they had prepared. "Thou hast made all things. Thou art the giver. Thou hast guarded me by day and night. Thou hast made the sun and moon and stars. Thou makest the rain, the thunder, the hail, and the snows. Thou hast given us souls that will never die."

He paused for just a moment here. He did not want to cry. Then, in a strong voice he went on, "*No-si-inan wah-kwing e-be-yon* (Our Father who art in Heaven). . ." All the way to the final whisper, "*Apanga.* (Amen.)"

It was late in the afternoon when he carved her name and then the date on the smooth gray bark of a beech tree that stood beside the grave. The letters stood out boldly.

M A R Y G O O D H U E
1 8 3 8

It was then he heard the owl. The owl would assist her spirit on its journey. He felt a rush of gratitude, knowing all was well.

* * *

The next day in the early morning he made his preparations that he, too, might leave. First, he bundled his possessions— the few that he'd brought with him when he came, the furs his efforts had obtained and those that she had given. He took his ledgers, filled now with his writing, and his ax and blanket. He had, of course, his flint and stone, his knife, and the coin for luck. He hesitated at the bundle, wrapped in its blue cloth. Was this the time to open it? She had said that he would know. He did not feel it strongly and he put it in his pack.

These things done, he began on the final chores. He swept the floor with hemlock branches and laid the broom away. He notched the day stick one last time—a hundred and forty-seven tallies, each one standing for one day and its companion night. He closed the door and latched it, knowing this was foolish. Nothing guarding nothing.

The difficult woods of winter were now turned into bowers. Small leaves graced the pleasant trees, and beneath his moccasins the forest floor was soft. Because he now had much weight on his back, he used a stout, dark walking stick. But it was more for balance than to lean upon.

In an hour's walk he reached the place where, in deep and trampled snow, Bad Pierre had lain. There was, of course, no trace of this. Shem picked himself a cowslip and stuck it in his belt.

Beaubien had taken the map of the territory. Although they'd cursed it often for its errors, there was much that was correct. Three days into his journey, Shem wished he had that map.

Although she'd said it "was not far," these three days of steady travel had not brought him to the village where he planned first to stop. Here he'd hoped to trade some of his furs for a light canoe. With a canoe he would not have to walk—except for the portages! Although he was so much stronger now, distances were hard for him to walk and would always be so. How far might it be, he wondered? Had Mary Goodhue misdirected him? Had he, still more likely, taken a false turn? The straps of his pack cut deeply as the old doubts settled in.

In the forest, dusk comes early, and the air turns cool. Aware that he was leaning heavily on his stick and that he was tired, Shem decided he would stop rather than press on. He looked about for a sheltered place and made his night's encampment as soon as one appeared.

As the day sounds changed to those of night, Shem, beside his quickly kindled fire, heard a wolf's long howl. Was it a sound of greeting or farewell? It had the same insistency as the wolf call he'd heard months ago when alone in the little cabin. Again it called, and nearer. He felt fear run along his arms and sensed there was something he must do, if only he understood.

And then, at once, he did. This was the time and this the place to receive the final gift. As when a puzzling question is resolved, ease replaced the agitation he had just endured.

The garment, when he laid the cloths aside, glowed in the fire's light. It was of the softest skins and rich with bright designs. It had been made while Mary Goodhue waited for her husband. Now she meant for Shem to wear it. This was what she wanted him to know: he, too, had made her happy.

When, through the ring of circling trees, he glimpsed a star in the dark of the western sky, Shem was filled with a sadness so intense it seemed to verge on joy. The wind came up and as suddenly was still. He gently refolded the garment and laid it in his pack. He heard the wolf, retreating now, deeper in the forest. Shem drew his blanket closer. It was good, at last, to sleep.

Next morning he knew with certainty that he would find the village. He had let himself be carried too far north. He corrected his course accordingly and soon his mocassined feet came on a trail that his eyes could not discover. The sun had barely shifted in the sky when the barking of a dog confirmed that he was making an approach to a village of some sort.

*   *   *

FROM THE NOTEBOOKS OF SHEM PERKINS
FOR MAY (JUNE?), 1838:

. . . I then continued on the trail and soon was greeted by a youth and the dog I had just heard.

"Bo'jour," I said. "Where is your village?" (using the Ottawan words). He seemed surprised and pleased by this, and responded in a friendly manner, calling on me to follow him and adjusting his pace to mine. On arriving at the camp I was pleasantly greeted by the father of my guide.

My bowl, at the evening meal, was heaped with meat and yellow broth and oil. I ate with relish—real at first, then feigned—as I thought of Mary Goodhue's teaching exactly on this point. I asked my hosts if they had seen or heard of the members of my party. Mr. Beaubien was known to them. But no, they said with much assurance, there had been no traders since the time of their return. In the winter, I pressed on, might they have come before? In the winter, who would know? They were not here to see! I joined, with as much good nature as I could, in the laughter at my own expense, and postponed the inquiry.

In the morning I traded one of my smaller pelts for all the meal that I could carry, a pair of mocassins, well made, some neips, and a buckskin shirt. This last was of less good quality, but it would suffice.

These small transactions persuaded me that these were honest fellows. I explained my need for a small canoe, 12 feet, and asked if any of their number might provide the same. This occasioned lively talk conducted in their tongue. Accustomed to Mary Goodhue's diction, I could not understand their speech, except for a scattered word or two; also their conclusion, which was negative.

On asking then if any of them knew where I might acquire a canoe, I was directed, cheerfully enough, to another village. In the morning I set out.

* * *

XVIII

By Trail and Bark Canoe

SHEM HAD HOPED that the next few days of travel would bring him to his canoe. Although these hopes were not fulfilled, his notes remain quite cheerful. He comments on the flowers he observes, giving the English equivalents of their Indian names. He passes an abandoned camp; the heaped up branches where they slept tell him how many men were there. The appearance of the ashes of their fire suggest that they roasted game. Disdainful of their bruiting about the circumstances of their stay, he concludes that the men were traders and not Ottawans. There are hunters in the forest now— mostly Indians returning to their fields from their winter quarters. Shem invites a squirrel to dinner, tactfully refraining, as he notes, from eating squirrel that night.

Indeed, what is most striking in these pages is Shem's good-humored energy, the lively interest he displays toward all that he surveys. And then this one notation: *I feel that I shall meet no harm. The one she named my brother is with me day by day.*

When Shem began his travels, wild strawberries were in

bloom. Before he had acquired his canoe, they were bearing fruit. In short, it was a matter of some weeks until he met success.

* * *

FROM: *THE MEMOIRS OF A PIONEER SON,* PRINTED BY HIMSELF. ONE COPY (#54) PRESENTED TO THE MILLFIELD HISTORICAL SOCIETY BY HIS DESCENDENTS

Chapter Twenty-seven

In Which I Acquire a Canoe and the Answer to Some Questions

The canoe which presently I obtained was better than I expected and less good than I hoped. It had been buried to protect it from the weather. When it had been fully excavated, I recognized its low and rounded ends as an indication of local origin. I saw that it had been well used and also much repaired. But being scarcely 12 feet long, it would be light in portages and easy to maneuver.

All this while I was staying at the camp of the Indians. No one, though I asked them plainly, could tell me aught of Good Pierre, or Beaubien, or Zozep. I had thought they might have passed this village, it being in a central plain, but this was not the case.

The reason that I stayed so long was to prepare the canoe itself for the certain adversity of the upstream journey which I would have to make. At times I had the aid of others; often I worked alone. Many was the patch I spoiled by seaming it too closely to the edge and many was the root I ruined in my attempt to win from it a fiber of good length. I believe that the repair of my canoe ought not to have taken more than several days. However, my inexperience did much to extend the work.

But perhaps it all went for the best. In the time that I stay'd there I learned much about the needs of my little craft. Also how to handle it should I need to navigate in shallow or rapid waters. Indian youths, about my age, were my amused instructors. From them I learned the strokes that I should need and how to know what lay ahead by observing the water's surface. If the water rilled beguilingly, I now took it as warning of craggy rock beneath. I recognized the stillness of the surface that overlies deep channels.

In canoeing I had found the one activity where my foot was no disadvantage! I long'd to make the most of it and dreamed of the day when I might be as accurate, strong, and graceful as the Indian boys and men.

Meanwhile I plied my cautious way and learned what I could from watching them. We became good friends.

When I left we swore to meet again, despite the great unlikelihood that we should ever do so.

* * *

Shem had left the tally stick behind. Now by his estimation it was early in July. On which one of these days, he wondered, had his countrymen engaged in their celebration of Independence Day? He remembered trying to explain its meaning and Mary Goodhue's vexed remark ending the discussion. If the wind blows here from Canada, she'd said, is that a British wind?

Had the Ellsworths come to Millfield for the day? Had Margaret worn her mother's brooch again? Had his own mother baked up pies, as she used to do? Thoughts of home were not infrequent through the sometimes sultry days. Yet in none of them did he guess that preparations for his sister's marriage were even then taking place!

True it was that Sophy and John Hall would marry in the last week of July, and Millfield seemed enlivened as the festivities approached. Nearly all participated in one way or another. For want of a church, the wedding would take place in the newly completed depot. This structure afforded the largest space in town but was rather bare. So, hours before the ceremony, the loving labor of many hands filled it with leafy branches and flowers of several sorts. The central aisle was improvised. But Sophy walked on it that day as if it had been ancient stone laid with crimson carpet.

Then, in a simple ceremony, the sweet vows were exchanged. All those present joined in song, and the new and radiant Mr. and Mrs. Hall passed through the open doorway to begin their wedded life.

Something else of importance happened on that day. The Fiddler had declared that when they came to dancing, he would play the tunes. From the moment that his bow first touched the strings, it seemed that all he could not say in words welled forth in the music. There were many tunes he had to play, and on he went, from one tune to another while the crowd before him danced at his command. Then, on a sudden, as so many years before, he passed the fiddle on midtune and when he caught his Lyddie's eye, he snapped her up to dance.

* * *

FIRST PAGE ONLY OF LETTER TO ANN (MRS. CHARLES) HALL
FROM LYDIA (MRS. THOMAS) PERKINS: SUBSEQUENT PORTIONS
ILLEGIBLE DUE TO WATER DAMAGE.

Millfield, Michigan
July 14, 1838

Dear Ann,

Your letter reached us very well and glad you are the same. In two weeks' time our Sophy is getting married. She talks of nothing else. Perhaps one day, we being kin through that, you will visit here. I think you would find it pleasant especially in the spring.

Millfield is now a station stop and Mr. P. works every day but Sunday at the depot here in town. Very convenient, as we are very near. He is well payed. There is considerable traffick both passenger and freight with more to be expected. On Independence Day we had a fine celebration, none injured I am glad to say, you would have enjoyed it.

I hope you heard the last of any talk about the merchant and myself. If not please tell them they are very wrong. You will know how to talk to them I hope as you are a teacher. Tell them it is wicked lies, no more. Amos Edwards was a good man, that I know, and a loyal friend. I did not know his private griefs, nor was he cause of mine . . .

* * *

An extended portage marked the end of the first part of Shem's journey. The next part would be easier as he'd be headed downstream with the current in his favor. Indeed,

Shem thought, some few days hence, it was the closest one could get to traveling as the gods must travel, with hardly any effort through surpassingly lovely scenes.

Once a heron kept him company. For miles the great bird flew ahead, beating its wings above the water as Shem plied his paddle, enraptured by the sight.

It was not until the river reached its end in Lake Huron's vast extent that Shem met other people, either Indian or white. The latter seemed the more surprised to find a young boy traveling alone. His story reassured them and was quickly told. Each time he ended with the query: and had they heard, did they know aught, of the trader, Mr. Beaubien? There was also a woodsman, called Zozep, and a boatman named Pierre?

Three times he asked to no avail. Then, one evening, a party of two canoes, each one passing 20 feet in length, joined him on the open beach where he had made his camp.

* * *

FROM THE NOTEBOOKS OF SHEM PERKINS:

Learned yesterday that Beaubien is dead, likewise Good Pierre. They were both good friends to me. May they rest in peace.

My informants were a trading party, who had the story from Zozep who, seemingly, was known to them through his mother's kin.

After Beaubien and the rest had left me at the cabin they had travelled southward and then somewhat east. Establishing a camp on the Grand River they enjoyed successful trading with the Chippewas. But Beaubien was taken ill. For days he seemed insensible, nor could he eat or drink. During this, the loudest of his men had vanished in the night. They did not need to tell me that this was Bad Pierre! Clearly he had reckoned me for dead and thought to claim for his own ends the stores left at the cabin. At least he had been foiled in this. Thereafter I expended no concern on his whereabouts.

Beaubien had presently recovered and they had stay'd through March. As soon as the ice was off the river, he, Zozep, and Good Pierre attempted the northward journey back to Mackinac. They had not travelled very far when the shallow river, swollen with melted snow, presented a course of rapids they had not anticipated. Their canoe was heavy and they had many furs. They did not wish to portage. Instead they attempted lining. They knew the danger of this course and, as would have been so typical of him, Beaubien assigned himself the position of greatest risk. The other two took stations on the shore, each equipped with a line by which to guide the imperilled boat. They proceeded bravely for a bit. Then it was a shifting wind that gusted and so caused their fate. The canoe was quickly overturned, Beaubien trapped beneath. Attempting rescue, Good Pierre had also lost his life. They were good men, both of them, but God's will be done.

Zozep, loyal to the last, recovered both the bodies and buried them on the spot. He said that when he turned away the dead men called out after him: adieu, Zozep, adieu.

My informants now insist that the place is haunted. When the wind is right, they say, one can hear them calling still: adieu, Zozep, adieu.

*   *   *

XIX

A Fair Peninsula

THE WELL-KNOWN STORY of Rip Van Winkle tells, by its very exaggeration, the emotions that are common to all travelers. Rip cries out, on coming home, "Everything's changed, and I'm changed."And whether one is gone but a week, or many years, one echoes his observation.

So Shem felt, too, on returning to Detroit after his long adventure.The passing months had indeed transformed the city that the boy had left! In well kept yards before the greater houses, seasonal flowers bloomed in beds and beans hung heavily from vines in leafy kitchen gardens. The waterfront was raucous now, and people in bright summer dress spilled from every shop and inn and gathered on the streets.

It was also true that Shem himself presented an altered mien. Instead of the pale demeanor of a clerk, his was the manner and complexion of one compelled by circumstance to be strong and self-reliant. His hair, queued back, was lightened by the sun. His stride was unashamed. Most of all, his

forthright air and his purposeful expression overcame the
least impression of disability.

"So the little rabbit has at last become the hare!" How the
comment startled him! But the tone was unmistakable, and
the speaker was Zozep.

What a greeting then took place as, with shouts and exclamations, they fell upon each other! Shem was hugged and
slapped upon the back! Zozep had to look at him! Had to
touch his hands and face and make Shem show the muscles
of his arms, hardened by the steady paddling of the recent
weeks. He swore that Shem was taller than he'd been a few
short months ago.

Zozep approved the buckskin shirt ("So, Shem, you are one
of ours!") and took in, without comment, the heavy walking
stick. His inspection traveled from Shem's hair to the mocassins on his feet.

"So," he said, reflectively, "so the boots are gone."

Then Shem explained, surprised to find it so, that he had
left the boots behind, not using them anymore. While the
summer sun blazed overhead the two recalled the silent, icy
days when a woodsman, quaintly named, despaired for a lame
and angry boy and had given him hare to eat.

Despite his joy at seeing Zozep once more, it was naggingly
on Shem's mind to call on Mr. Prentice and give him his report. Then Zozep would go along—what else!—and as they
walked Shem begged his friend to tell of all that happened
since they saw each other last.

* * *

. . . as he had heard that I had died Mr. Prentice was quite visibly surprised when I made my appearance at his office door. He, poor man, had regretted many times my assignment to a wilderness position and blamed himself for my death.

I assured him I was very much alive and gave him a written inventory of the trade goods left behind. I then went on to tell him of the events which had befallen all the party and which are set down here. Mr. Prentice listened well enough, but when he moved to end the conversation I could delay no longer in coming to my point.

"Beyond the return of the ledgers, sir," said I, "I've come to collect my pay."

"Pay?" said he, seeming very much surprised. "As not one fur has yet been brought in trade, what can there be in pay?"

I answered him quite smartly but meant no offense. "I was not engaged as a trader, sir, and have kept the ledgers as you have seen just now."

"So you have, lad, so you have." At which he leaned back in his chair and thoughtfully stroked his lips. At last he took, from a drawer beneath his desk, a small locked wooden box. He opened it and, after a moment's search, handed me a bank note for some twenty dollars.

"Thank you, sir," said I to him, thinking there must be rhyme or reason to it; I had left home for bank notes, and was now with bank notes paid!

As one man to another we shook hands. Then, even as I

turned to leave, he added that promotion would be mine should I wish re-employment with the company.

"God speed!" he called after me, and again the small halls echo'd. But now it was with friendly greeting, not the slow and labored measures of a lame boy's boots.

* * *

When Shem, in giving his report, had mentioned Mary Good-hue's name, Zozep looked at him amazed and somewhat disbelieving. He would have been no more surprised had Shem been to Washington and dined with Mr. Van Buren, who was then the president. Zozep had heard of Mary Goodhue; who, indeed, had not! Long ago, on Mackinac, he had heard the stories of this woman. No one knew as much as she of the healing arts. So many came to see her that some she turned away.

"We were friends," Shem told him simply. "There was that at first."

Now Zozep expressed renewed surprise. It was said that she befriended many but took none as friend. It was said that she had sealed her heart when her husband died. He had been a noted hunter; a warrior, as well. Pontiac and Tecumseh were no more brave than he.

"We were friends," Shem said again. "At the end she said that I was fit to be his kin."

That night they stayed at a public house filled with woodsmen, trappers, guides—all friends of Zozep's, it seemed, by their fervent greetings. Zozep was so proud of Shem and, telling fragments of his story, made the boy's lone journey and return the exploit of the hour. Men kept crowding close to hear Shem's clear-voiced recital. He did not tell them everything, and some he painted in a bit, such as his retrieval of the coin from Bad Pierre. Among the men were some to whom Pierre had shown the coin and boasted how he'd come to take it from the sleeping boy. Now they laughed aloud to hear the final turn to the story of the coin of French design.

Shem enjoyed the approval of the men, but it also conferred an eminence that he felt he must decline. When the two of them were alone once more, he said softly to Zozep: "In the time with Mary Goodhue, when she died and needed me, there was nothing else to do and no one else to do it. Indeed, I had been glad enough for that, but everyone had gone."

"That is right," Zozep agreed, reminding Shem by his diction of his beloved friend. "Cowards speak of courage; the brave do what they must."

Shem raised his head and nodded. If Zozep said the praise was well deserved, he, Shem, would accept it.

"And so," Zozep concluded, "it all went for the best. Beginning"—and he glanced at Shem—"beginning with the rabbits Zozep caught for you!"

Just before he fell asleep Shem remembered drowsily the stories his mother told. It seemed there was always a foolish lad and a wise but ragged woman. Carelessly coming to her relief, the boy would find himself a hero, receiving a gift of magic beans for his modest favor.

Then it was morning and time to say good-bye. Shem

pressed the name of Millfield on his friend, fervently hoping
that Zozep would find him there one day. They clapped each
other on the back with cries and exclamations. Then Zozep,
with hands upon Shem's shoulders, held him out at arm's
length to look at him once more. He tried to speak but found
no words, turned, and walked away. Shem watched him till
he disappeared. Then he turned the corner and walked north
on Jefferson.

He had in mind to bring each one a gift and used the last
of Mary Goodhue's furs to obtain the things he needed. Had
she not wished to see them? He felt she would approve.

In a nearby shop he bought a length of cloth that he
thought would please his mother. For Annie a book with edi-
fying stories, but sparing the deaths of martyrs, and some
pretty pictures of girls and boys at play. For his father, what
to do? Anguished with embarrassment, he chose a beaver hat.
It was the kind the legislators wore—Shem had seen enough
of them!—and the wealthy gentlemen in the big hotels.

Across the street from the capitol, he stepped inside a public house for a meal and a bit to drink. Through windows shin-
ing with real glass he watched officials come and go and
caught, with real excitement, a glimpse of the governor! A
man still in his twenties, as Shem knew, he looked even
younger amidst august companions competing for his eye.

The scene, when the little crowd had passed, seemed so
plain and ordinary; no one knowing—nor could they know—
the extent to which this was, for Shem, a marked and special
day! *Si quaeris peninsulum amoenam*—well, it had been fair

to him. And now, as he looked about himself, there was much to delight his eye.

Suddenly Shem remembered something: Margaret Ellsworth on the day her father's house was raised. She had looked so new and changed but when he'd tried to speak of it—"That brooch, it was so pretty on your dress!"—she refused the compliment. "It isn't even mine," she'd said, "but my mother's, she let me wear."

He would buy her one right now! Then she could wear it all she wished and, if ever someone noted it, could say, "Yes, it was a gift to me, from my friend, Shem Perkins."

The one he chose was silver, all entwined. The proprietor said it was directly from New York and the very latest style. Shem nodded his appreciation. He doubted, though, that Margaret Ellsworth knew or cared enormously for fashions in the East.

It was noon now on the following day. Shem sweltered in the heat. He had put himself in line for a lot of upstream work and was glad that he had taken time to load the canoe with care. It now rode evenly and low, the prow less likely to be caught by overhanging trees.

There were good fields here beside the river, and many pleasing homes. A bridge crossed to a settlement, reminding him of Millfield's bridge, and he noted with approval a pier at which boats rode. *Amoenam*, he repeated to himself: pleasant, fair, and good.

He began to think about his father. What might he be doing, right now at this minute? He'd not thought much of their last days together. They were dark, unhappy times. Would that be behind them, or there to be resumed? For the first time it occurred to him that probably he should have written, ought to have sent some word. Conversely, and with some surprise, he realized he knew nothing—good or ill—of happenings in Millfield since he'd gone away. A cloud of worry passed before the sun of his happiness. He paddled beneath it silently. Then it burned away.

The real sun on his neck was strong, but the day went well. He hardly stopped to eat at noon, and that night, sheltered, safe, and dry, slept beneath his overtuned canoe close on the river's bank. His bundled goods were close at hand, beside his gun and paddle.

It would have surprised Shem, had he known, that even then in camps and public rooms men were passing on his stories, adding a few embellishments to lend the proper spirit. So it was, in times to come, that one might hear of a crippled lad whom Mary Goodhue healed before she died, how he had assisted her, and how she had bestowed on him the secrets of the forest and her most magic lore.

The sky, when he awoke next day, was rumpled and iridescent. It looked like the inside of a shell that Shem had seen once, brought from a foreign shore. Lavender tones suffused the pinks and golds, and as Shem watched the entire eastern sky turned pearly with new light. Then, when the sun thus heralded appeared, Shem took it as a signal and began his day. It was time for the preparations he had planned so long.

First, a cleansing in the river: hair and hands, whole body

washed and scrubbed, using sand to do it. The water had a freshness at this hour. He smelled the freshness of the water on his naked body. Then, while the soft air made him dry, he unwrapped the bundle, Mary Goodhue's final gift. He laid it gently on the grass. Everything must be clean this day—down to the underclothes he wore. Nothing old or worn or mended would he wear this day.

Around him now the light was strong; everything was touched by it and it touched him, too. He put on his trousers, his neips and mocassins. Finally, hair well smoothed and tied, he was ready for the shirt. He stood to put it on. The sun had warmed it where it lay. It seemed it must be made to his own measure, so perfectly did it fit him, so supple and so light. Slowly, with instinctive gesture, he spread his arms and turned his face to find the risen sun. The sun struck fully on his figure, blessing the beautiful garment by which he himself felt blessed.

Long to be remembered, the actual moment passed. Shem cleared away his little camp, placed his belongings thoughtfully, and felt the familiar yielding and return as the canoe received his weight and then regained its balance. How he loved this little boat of his! Gently, fondly, he guided it beyond a tree trunk, half submerged, and moved toward a deeper channel. He adjusted his grip on the paddle and placed the first full stroke.

XX

The Place from Whence We Started

SHEM HAD LIKED MUSIC WELL ENOUGH but was not a singer. Once, after joining in the Sunday hymns with all his school-boy's energy, he'd been asked to mouth the words hereafter but not attempt the tunes. So it was some surprise to him that his voice, which recently had deepened, was also much more true.

Paddling, he had sung the songs learned by listening to Zozep and the two Pierres. These were mostly sad and rhythmic ballads. Love went unrequited and maidens' hearts were cruel. Then he commenced on the songs his father played. He had never tried to learn them, but he seemed to know them all! And he sang the one song Mary Goodhue taught; the one by which, so long ago, a hunter bravely signaled that he was coming home.

"That would be the death song?" Shem had asked.

"No," she'd said, "a song to make one strong for that which is to be."

* * *

148

Shem was coming closer now. Just how near he did not know, but the river, as it flowed between its banks, seemed somehow more familiar. It widened, rippled, curved. He swept beneath the bridge, passed the gristmill with its pond, and the first of Millfield's yards.

The Fiddler, despite all indications, had never given up the hope that Shem was coming home. At first he thought this might be in the spring, perhaps in time for planting. Then, when spring went by without a word, he amended his prediction. With summer well along by now, his hopes were pinned on autumn, making it one full year!

He thought if the boy was working on a farm he'd want to see the harvest through, and this would be expected. Thus it is that, lacking information, one constructs a scheme for one's beliefs and presently confers on them their own reality.

Indeed, his son was the subject of his remarks as he walked out this evening with his friend George Howe. After the bad times that they'd had, what with the rowdies, and the wedding sheets, and what had come thereafter, the Howe and Perkins families had become good friends. There were some who gave the printer little time on account of his beliefs. Tom could not see it so. In fact, the printer was the one who seemed best to understand the father's hopes for his son, Shem, his griefs and disappointments.

"I always tried," Tom told him now, "to treat him straight, the same as any other; strict and fair, I treated him, and made no room for pity. Oh, it broke my heart sometimes! But I didn't want to treat him easy, and his mother, she agreed. We feared he'd get expecting it from others or feeling sorry for himself—"

"No," the printer commented, "that would be the worst of all. I kind of wish I'd known him though—funny, he never asked of me and all that time he was looking for paid work—"

This was embarrassing to Tom, and he didn't know what to say. He wondered if he should explain that Mrs. Perkins, at that time, had strictly cautioned Shem against connection with the printer.

"Would you believe," he asked his friend, deciding to change the subject, "we're past two hundred and fifty dollars nearly every day we run in passenger fares alone? But hush," he said. "What's that?"

There could be heard quite clearly now the sound of a distant voice. It seemed to come from down the river, and Tom knew with a certainty that no white person had composed the melody it offered. It raised their skin in gooseflesh on their arms; amazement and alarm were mixed in their surprised emotions.

They stared downstream as a small canoe came around the bend. It appeared to be an Indian's canoe by the way it rode the water and the style of paddling used. It carried but a single figure whose identity was hard to guess; they could not see it clearly in the failing light.

The two men waited, silent and intent. The song came to an end. Without a pause or hesitation, but seeming to gather up resolve, the singer's voice burst forth anew, exuberant and strong.

"We're all a-marching to Quebec—"

"Shem!" his father shouted.

Then he was running toward his son, stumbling along the riverbank with its tangled roots.

The Ellsworths had gone down to call the very day word came around that the Perkins boy was home. This was the visit of her parents, which perhaps was just as well. Margaret, in her pale-green dress sprigged with flowers of some sort, looked so different from the Margaret-in-the-woods whom Shem best remembered. Shem felt shy and instantly regretted the little gift he'd brought. On her side, unbeknownst to him, she felt much the same. When so often to console herself, Margaret had remembered Shem, the boy she had remembered was the boy who went away, a gentle lad whose gait and carriage were difficult to behold. She had pitied him, to her shame, and, in time, had come to feel a sisterly affection.

The new Shem moved her differently, he with his stories of the woods amidst difficult circumstances. He was talking of an Indian. Mary Goodhue was her name and Shem, by the way he chose his words, seemed to think the world of her. She, Margaret, must seem foolish to him now. What had she to offer? Why did it matter so?

Margaret, with her hair well tied, sat with her hands correctly in her lap. Then it was time to say good night politely to Shem's parents. Shem feared that he had wearied her. She had not said a word. He watched the Ellsworths' wagon as it moved on up the street.

It was exactly one week later that Shem made his visit. He was inclined a hundred times to abandon his intentions. But, for a hundred times *and one*, he determined to go on. He saw, as he approached the house, that she was in the yard. He raised his head and put his shoulders back. Had not Mary Goodhue said that it was so one must approach and whether the settlement be that of enemy or friend.

"Here," he said abruptly. "I fetched it in Detroit." He had not meant to blurt it out, but neither had he considered that she'd just be waiting there. Now he must untie the knot with which he had secured it.

But Margaret's mind was elsewhere. There was something she must say.

"Shem," she said, remembering the day she'd so offended him, "Shem, just now I didn't notice. I mean I really didn't notice—"

"Didn't notice what?" he asked, in genuine confusion.

"Oh, you know," she said distressed. Would she never get it right? Because here, now, he was handing her his gift, wrapped in a little paper square and sealed with a drop of wax.

She opened the corners one by one, extending the pleasure of the secret and, at the same time, putting off the moment of its revelation: would it please or disappoint?

"Shem," she said. "It's beautiful!"

It was the sort of gift men brought to girls whom they were courting.

* * *

LETTER FROM SOPHIA P. HALL TO CATHERINE HALL:

Millfield, Michigan
August 27, 1838

My very dearest Catherine,

Once again, good news! My brother Shem is home once more—he is well and quite unharmed; indeed is quite improved. You can imagine the good effect on our mother's health! Shem now wears *mocassins* on his feet and walks with such assurance that one hardly notes the lameness that once smote the eye. Under the mocassins he wears the folded squares of blanketing the Indians call neips. He affects the wilderness buckskin shirt and its long hairstyle as well. The change, I will say, is quite complete! But I must say they become him well—or is it the sights that he has seen, the hardships he endured? Suffice it that my brother Shem has returned quite handsome and in ways I had not guessed!

After a brief employment as a clerk, he spent six months in the wilderness, much of it alone. However, for a time he was the sole companion of an Indian, a woman and very old. It seems that he was with her when she died and attended to her needs. He firmly believes a kinship with her people. He speaks especially of her husband who is long deceased. John, who is quite fond of Shem, thinks it much less odd than I and it may be he is right.

I think it most unlikely that my brother return to school. He is working with the printer and does very well ($4 a week). I believe my parents had favoured his preparation for teaching at the school. But no, he would have none of this. They have not pressed the matter.

John and I continue very happy, debating shall he build a mill or enter into partnership with one that is established. Whatever course he takes in that, we shall need a larger house. I estimate our child will come before the winter's out. As yet it is not showing. I blush to tell the news.

Please write and tell me all *your* news. I dote on every line you write and please tell all of those at home, whomever it is you visit next, they are in our daily thoughts. We beg we remain in theirs.

I hope this finds you in good health, my oldest, dearest, cherished friend—and now my niece by marriage! I send you the affection and the greetings of your *aunt,*

S.H.

We feel very fortunate as we have not had the fever and the chills and are near the end of summer. John thinks 'tis the setting of our house, well beyond the river in a clean, dry situation. My father had a small recurrence but already it has abated.

* * *

That year it took a full three weeks from the first bright flash of color till the hillsides blazed farewell to the summer season. Shem was enormously content; so never mind that in the East banking houses tumbled and financial prospects dimmed. If he had been successful as a clerk, Shem loved the work that fell to him as a printer's boy! And Sophy turned out wrong about one thing: Shem did go to school.

He went because the printer said he must. "In this work, Shem, you have to know as much as you are able: grammar to correct your texts, and rhetoric to improve them. Arithmetic to attend to your accounts, and logic—you will need that, son, to attend to you!"

But the reason Shem remained a scholar was of quite a different sort. Margaret, too, attended school, walking the two miles into town to sit in the drafty parlor of the teacher's house. In all there were fourteen pupils from the infant abecedarians to Shem and Margaret. They would have liked the kitchen better, with its ample fireplace. Instead they were accommodated with chill formality.

Shem and Margaret, combined, formed the entire Latin class and the oldest rank of students. After the spare economy of the graceful Ottawan tongue, Latin, so oppressively detailed, was burdensome to Shem. They took to studying together, reviewing and repeating the endless lists of verbs.

Now it was deep winter. But even when the roads were drifted white and Margaret floundered on her way to school, Shem, in the snowshoes he had made, reached her home with ease.

Heads bent to their lesson books, they sat at the hearthside table or stretched out close beside the fire where the floor was warm. There they must be wary of the sparks; Margaret's skirt had more than once been scorched. But the cozy pleasures of the hearth were more than worth the dangers.

How different was this gentle scene from that rude hearth where, not so long ago, Shem had knelt to start a fire, desperate for warmth. Shem reflected, as he often did, on the days with Mary Goodhue. They had begun to sort themselves: there were those when she'd been well, and the ones when she was not. At first he thought more often of the small and quiet hours when, deep in dream, she'd left him. Lately, he thought more about the many days of merriment and jokes.

Startling Margaret by speaking Ottawan, "What have you there?" he asked her. "Where do you live? Bo'jour! Good morning! My name it is Shem."

So his instruction had commenced, and so he began his teaching of Margaret Ellsworth now.

"What is your name?"

("Margaret Ellsworth is my name.")

"What have you there?"

("I have my book and pen.")

"She is wise and beautiful—"

("Oh, Shem, do you stop it now!")

"He is handsome." (Laughing.)

One day, several weeks thereafter, he amused her with his imitation of their Latin lesson book. The reference, now, was Ottawan, but the pompous intonation was borrowed from the book.

"The reflexive tense," he solemnly declared, "is formed by placing the syllable *ne* before the verb in question, and *ego* after it."

She had to laugh aloud at this. "Oh, don't do that, Shem," she said. "Just say it, so it's right."

"All right, then. *Sageau*, I love."

"*Ne sageau ego*," she answered. "I am loved."

* * *

Spoken with a scholar's innocence, her words, before many years had passed, proved to be prophetic. By the time Shem came of age, the two were promised to each other, and the fact that she was nearly two years older never came between them. Their marriage was well celebrated, and all this time Shem continued with his work at Mr. George Howe's press.

When Shem's first child, a healthy girl, was born, his fond employer marked the glad event by making Shem his partner in the printing shop. Down came the old sign, up went the new. As HOWE AND PERKINS, PUBLISHER AND PRINTER the business grew and prospered, as did the town itself.

Shem's influence as a publisher was great, for the newspaper office, in those years, was a place where opinion flourished and judgment yet held sway. Well respected by the town, rewarded by public office, Shem became known throughout the state for his numerous services as a citizen.

As for Shem and Margaret, they lived in good health and mutual affection to their fiftieth wedding day. Their children came with their husbands, wives, and children and the children of these children. Sophy, now the Widow Hall, was there, and Annie, who was getting on in years, and those whose births and marriages, successes and tribulations, Shem had reported faithfully in his weekly paper. As no man's life is lived apart from others, so an occasion of this sort acknowledges and appreciates more than its guests of honor.

It is getting on toward evening now; the platters are nearly emptied and the icy pitchers drained. The daughters and the daughters-in-law begin to clear the tables. The crowd begins to separate, preparing its farewells.

The story, in time , is all that stays; and all that stays is story.

Author's Note
& Acknowledgments

This book was supposed to be about New England, with a peddler as its hero. That the story did not turn out that way attests to the liveliness of fiction; as capricious as a diviner's rod, it points its own direction.

On settling myself in Michigan, as it were, I read more books on its history and traditions than can be cited here. Especially useful were those by Bruce Catton[1] and Willis F. Dunbar[2], and Andrew J. Blackbird's 1897 *History of the Ottawa and Chippewa Indians of Michigan*[3] with its grammar and glossary of the Indian languages.

Although many near-by libraries and communities have excellent collections of material on regional history, I am particularly indebted to the Bentley Library of the University of Michigan, which is wonderful because its holdings are so extensive, and to the Ypsilanti Historical Society, which is wonderful because of its intimacy.

Always it was the pioneers' own accounts that interested me the most. Often their letters were difficult to read and

159

curiously punctuated if compared with modern practice. Until I had read it several times, I did not understand "Fanney has lost A daughter Cate is her name."[4] With their actual rhythms in my ear, as well as those of treatises and texts and nineteenth-century journals, I wrote, whole cloth, the letters and accounts which appear throughout the book. I have given in context the sources for the two authentic quotations: description of the ague, Chapter V, page 33, and comments on wildcat banking, Chapter VI, page 37. The day-by-day descriptions of weather, Chapters IX and XVI, pages 61 and 120 respectively, are also *bona fide*, having been taken from notes by Bela Hubbard, a cartographer and explorer whose extensive activities in the region began in the 1830's.

"The Episode of Indian Justice" reported in Chapter XII is adapted from an eyewitness account given by Gurdon S. Hubbard in an essay entitled "Incidents in the Administration of Indian Justice"[5]. In virtually identical form the same material comprises a chapter of his autobiography. The actual incident appears to have occurred in 1819, but I have taken the liberty of placing the fictional episode at a somewhat earlier date.

The prayer commencing with the words "[g]reat good author of life" is the work of Jane (Mrs. Henry Rowe) Schoolcraft. Written in the Chippewa, which was her first language, it was translated by its author and published in Mr. Schoolcraft's classic work *The American Indian*[6].

Of the many persons who helped me with this work I should like especially to thank Marian Worden Gotshall for her interest at a crucial time in the book's development and for making available to me certain family documents and records; Wesley and Eleanor Andrews, who read the book in manuscript and gave me the great benefit of their personal and scholarly familiarity with the Ottawan heritage and tradition; Stephen Blos and Sarah Innes, my son and daughter-in-law, who commented firmly and usefully on the first completed draft; and Peter Blos, Jr., my husband, for his insight and forbearance. It was he who, with characteristic generosity, gave me an early reference book, a work whose author's sentiments accord so closely with my own that I can do no better in concluding than to repeat them here.

No one can be more sensible than myself of the deficiency of the present volume. . . . This plea is put in to abate the severity of criticism which might be urged against any inaccuracies that may be discovered, either in point of fact or literary execution.[7]

JOAN W. BLOS
Ann Arbor, Michigan
April 8, 1985

1. Catton, Bruce. *Michigan: A Bicentennial History.* New York: Norton, 1976.
2. Dunbar, Willis F. *Michigan: A History of the Wolverine State.* Grand Rapids, Michigan: Eerdmans, 1965.
3. Blackbird, Andrew J. *A History of the Ottawa and Chippewa Indians of Michigan.* Ypsilanti, Michigan, 1897.
4. Fanney (Fanny?) has lost a daughter. Cate (Kate?) is her name.
5. Hubbard, Gurdon S. "Incidents in the Administration of Indian Justice." *Michigan Historical and Pioneer Collections,* III, pp. 127-129.